Violent Circle: Book Three

S.M. Shade

Cover art by Ally Hastings at Starcrossed Covers.
Interior formatting by Angela at That Formatting Lady.

Dedication

This book is dedicated to Veronica. Since I used your name, I guess Neal belongs to you. Sorry, Colette. #NealbelongstoV

Chapter One

Veronica

Have you ever had the crap scared out of you by a sigh? It doesn't seem possible, does it? That a little, quiet breath could cause someone to jump like they've been touched by a live wire and almost pee themselves. If you have trouble believing such a thing, you've never been a parent.

The sweet little love of my life, who I occasionally want to duct tape to a chair, stands beside my bed, giggling at my reaction. Why do kids do that? Just stand by your bed, all creepy and quiet, staring at you until you open your eyes?

"Aiden, you aren't supposed to wake me up until the clock says seven, remember? You're supposed to stay in bed."

"I didn't wake you up. I was quiet and waited for you to wake up on your own." He climbs over me like I'm a jungle gym, and I bite back a curse when his elbow jabs me in the nipple.

Stellar start to the day.

He stretches his little body out beside me, tucks his arms behind his head, and closes his eyes. I say a quick prayer to any god of single mothers that may be listening for him to fall back to sleep. I just need a few more minutes. Or an hour. An hour would be bliss.

I pull my covers over him, and I'm just starting to drift off again when I feel his warm palm against my cheek. "Mom," he whispers. “The clock says seven, and I might die if I don’t eat pancakes.”

A snort of laughter jumps out of me, and I drag myself to a sitting position. “I don’t think anyone ever died from a lack of pancakes, Ade.”

He pulls his knees up and rests his chin on them, giving me a serious look. “Do you really want to risk it?”

This kid. I swear, he’s too damned smart for his own good. It’s easy to forget he’s just getting ready to turn five because he acts like such a little man sometimes. You know, right before he does something like trying to shave the local stray cat because it looked hot with all that fur. Poor thing has a bare stripe right down its back.

“Nope, let’s get you some pancakes. Blueberry or chocolate chip?”

He bounds out of bed and streaks down the hallway, his voice carrying behind him. “Chocolate chiiip!” I’d better get moving before he decides to start without me.

Aiden watches me from his stool at the counter while I cook his pancakes, jabbering away the entire time. “Are Neal and Bailey going to come to my birthday party?”

I slide the pancakes onto a plate, and set it in front of him, along with a glass of milk. “Yes, they’ll be there.” Along with half the neighborhood from what I’m hearing. We’ve only lived here on Violet Circle for about two months, but everyone treats us as if they’ve known us forever. The sign may have been vandalized to say Violent Circle, but my experience so far has been positive.

It’s a strange neighborhood, full of eccentric people. There’s no denying that, but they stick together like family, and Aiden and I could really use the support right now.

“I like Bailey. She’s nice.”

“I’m glad. She likes you too.”

“Everybody likes me except Eddie, and I don’t care because he sucks.”

“Aiden!” I exclaim, turning away to hide my smile. “That’s not nice.”

He shrugs, taking a bite of his food. “He’s not nice. He says he's my boss cause he lives at the hotel and I only visit. I don't like him."

The kid really is a little monster, but he's only eight, and it's understandable that he'd have some problems. A cheap hotel isn't a place to raise a kid. Not that I'm judging his family. I know how hard things can be.

I take a seat across from him. "He's not your boss."

"I know."

"Would you like to live at the hotel?"

He blanches. "No way! I love my room. He has to sleep in the bed next to his parent's bed. And he can't have a lot of toys because there's nowhere to put them."

"He's having a hard time then, isn't he? You know how you get grouchy when you're upset? He probably feels that way a lot. It's not right that he's mean to you, but I want you to be nice to him anyway. Sometimes being nice to someone can make them feel better. You might be the only person who does that for him."

Aiden chews his lip, a habit we share when we're thinking or nervous. "But what if he's mean to me again?"

"Then come find me and we'll do something about it."

"Okay, I'll be nice." He swallows his last bite and drains his glass of milk.

"Go get dressed and pick out some toys and books for today. It's only a half day, and we'll get lunch on the way home, okay?" I ruffle his hair. He needs a haircut.

His eyes brighten. "Can we go to Carl's and get a shake?"

"Sounds good to me."

He races off to dress and pack his little backpack.

I hate that I have to drag him to work with me every day, but I don't have a choice. It won't be for much longer. Next fall, he'll start Kindergarten, and I'll be able to work days without worrying about him. Fortunately, the couple who own the hotel are fine with me bringing him along. There's always a few empty rooms where he can watch T.V., play his handheld game, read, or play with his toys. He's never too far away from me for me to hear him. Sometimes he trails along behind me from room to room as well. After two months, all the regular guests know him, and he knows his boundaries. I'm grateful for the small adjacent playground, so he doesn't have to be cooped up for hours, but on days like this, he's stuck inside.

I do a quick clean up from breakfast, grab a breakfast drink for myself, and guzzle it while I toss on my jeans and a tee shirt. It only takes me a few minutes to throw my hair up into a messy bun, brush my teeth, and wash my face. I don't bother to shower until after work. The rooms can be gross, so by the time I get home, I can't wait to wash away the grime.

The street is quiet when we leave since most people are just waking up. Ice cold rain falls through the mist hanging in the air, and I shiver as I buckle my seat belt. "You should've worn your big coat like I did," Aiden pipes up from the backseat.

"Yes, I should have." What can I say? Sometimes the kid is smarter than me.

The hotel isn't far away, and we pull into the lot less than ten minutes later. Most of the parking spots are empty, and I'm not surprised. This hotel caters mostly to boaters and fisherman when the weather is nice. Icy rain doesn't make people want to hit the lake.

Ruby, one of the clerks and daughter of the owners, smiles at us when we come in. "Aiden! I have something for you."

I swear, Aiden makes friends wherever he goes, and he has my employers and their family eating out of his hand. "Hi Ruby!" He bounds over to her, his eyes widening as she produces a DVD of his favorite cartoon.

"Botkids! Mom, look!"

"Someone left it in a room last week. No one called to claim it, so it's all yours." She looks up at me. "He can hang out here if you want and watch it in the lobby."

"Thank you. Just text if he pesters you." I wiggle my cell at her before looking down at my grinning son. "What do you say, Ade?"

"Thank you! And you look pretty! Hubba Bubba!" he exclaims, then darts off to pop the DVD into the player in the small lobby. He flops onto the couch, kicks off his shoes, flings his backpack to the floor, and props his feet on it.

Ruby glances at me, and we both break into laughter. "Where did he get hubba bubba from?"

"Pretty sure he meant hubba hubba, and I have a suspicion." It involves the group of young college guys who live down the street in an apartment the neighbors have dubbed Frat Hell. He told me Noble taught him how to talk to pretty girls.

She hands me a list of rented rooms. "It's pretty light today because of the rain. The only ones who haven't checked out yet are 110 and 112. Most of the regulars have their Do Not Disturb signs out, as usual."

The regulars—meaning guests who stay a few times a month and the two families and two residents who live here full time—generally keep the Do Not Disturb signs out on weekends when they don't want to be awakened early. They don't need us to clean every day, so I tend to do their rooms once or twice per week.

As much as I'd like the extra hours, I'm happy to leave early today. Since I asked off for Aiden's birthday, I have a rare three days off in a row coming up and I'm eager to get to it.

I hook the ring with the master key on my belt loop and fill my travel cup with coffee before heading to the housekeeping office. Office isn't the most accurate way to describe it. It's a long room with two carts sitting inside.

Shelves line the walls, stacked high with towels and bedding. Bins nearly overflow with tiny soaps, shampoos, plastic cups, ice containers, and all that other stuff you find in a two-star hotel room. A musty smell permeates the place, originating from the large sink in the corner. It doesn't seem to matter how much bleach I dump down that drain, it always smells like unwashed ass.

I load up a cart with everything I need and push it out into the breezeway. On days like this, I really wish I'd chosen a hotel with interior hallways and entrances. The bitter cold cuts through me, and it doesn't help that the wind keeps gusting, allowing the rain to reach me in waves as I park the cart as close to the brick wall as I can. There's enough of an awning to keep the stuff dry.

Shivering, I open the two empty rooms and the door connecting them. Nothing looks too bad, just the regular mess I'm accustomed to finding; a half empty pizza box on the table, a trash can overflowing with soda cans and wrappers, wet towels on the bathroom floor. I can knock these out in no time.

The sheets get stripped from both beds and added to the pile of wet towels headed for the laundry room. The owner's other daughter, Mia, comes in during the afternoon to wash the linens so that isn't part of my job. I remove all the trash, spray down the bathrooms, remake the beds with fresh sheets, and vacuum the floors. By the time I'm done with that, all I have to do is wipe down the bathrooms and restock everything. A quick peek in the microwaves show me they don't need cleaned, and same goes for the mini fridges. A spritz of air freshener and I'm out the door. I love rooms like this. So easy.

The next few rooms are pretty much the same. One bathroom is pretty gross, with piss everywhere except the toilet, but I expected it since the lady staying here had two boys about Aiden's age. They aren't known for their aim. Still, it doesn't take long to clean.

I'm down to my last two rooms. One is a stayover who will be here a second night, so all I need to do is clean the bathroom, dump the trash, and restock the towels, but the other is a checkout. And apparently, they're waiting until the last minute to leave.

I take a quick break to check on Aiden, who is playing a board game with Eddie in the lobby, and then tap on the stayover guest's door. "Housekeeping!" I call. They don't answer, and there's no car parked outside the room, so I unlock the door and step inside.

Now, this is always a tense moment. I can't count the number of bare asses, naked schlongs, and uncovered cooters I've been flashed since I've had this job. Most of the time it's an accident, but occasionally, there will be a pervert who gets off on flashing the housekeeper. Fortunately, the bed is empty.

I open the bathroom door, but suddenly remember I forgot to grab the toilet cleanser. I make it about three steps back toward my cart before a high-pitched scream fills the room and something slams into my butt, knocking me down on the carpet.

It happens so fast, I'm not sure what just occurred. I assume someone was in the bathroom, but she didn't have to knock me down. "I'm sorry!" I shout, getting to my feet. I'm barely standing when the scream rings out again, and I'm rushed by a pile of gray fur.

What the actual fuck?

Panic grabs me, and I don't give the monster a second look as I dart from the room, slamming the door behind me. Max, the maintenance man, hears me yell and sees me holding the door shut as if whatever is inside may be able to pick locks.

"Veronica? What's going on?"

"There's some deranged, screaming animal in there! It sounded human, but all I saw was hair. It knocked me down when I opened the bathroom door. I'm not going back in there. It's a mutant! Or a Chupacabra!" I've never heard of a Chupacabra in Indiana, but who knows?

Max snorts with laughter. "Someone probably locked their dog in the bathroom and it was eager for some company when you opened the door." Max shakes his head at me, a smile on his face. He's around fifty years old and has worked here for the last ten of them so I imagine he's seen everything.

"It wasn't a dog."

He sticks his hand out for the key, and I hand it over, taking a few steps back as he unlocks the door again.

"Hey, puppy, don't be scared," he coos, entering the room.

He doesn't exit with that confidence.

In fact, he barely makes it inside before he's on his ass. A mass of dirty gray hair tramples over him and runs into the parking lot with another blood curdling scream. This time I get a better look at it.

"It's a goat!" I announce.

"It's going to be a dead goat," Max grumbles, getting to his feet.

The goat rushes over to the field beside the hotel and starts munching on the grass. "Aw, poor thing. I guess it was hungry."

Max stares at it. "It's starving and filthy. I'll go call Mike and see how he wants to handle this. Animal Control should probably get involved."

"It might run off."

Max chuckles. "Then let it go. I'm not chasing it, so it can knock me on my ass again."

Max heads off to call the manager, and I duck back inside the room. As you can expect from someone who would keep a goat in a hotel room, the place isn't clean.

I've had some gross rooms in the past. Puke on the floor, shit on the wall beside the toilet, towels soaked in too many body fluids to tell what's what, but this is the first time I've seen a pile of goat shit in a bathtub.

Mike generally calls in a local crime scene cleanup crew that's qualified to clean up bodily fluids and hazards if it's bad. This is bad. Along with the shit in the tub, the goat walked through it at some point, so the whole bathroom is covered. When I let it out, it ran around the room, dragging its nasty hooves over everything.

The bed, carpet, and tiny loveseat have brown tracks covering them. This is so not in my job description. I back out and head down to the office.

"Mom! Is there really a goat in a room?" Aiden asks, excitement ringing in his voice.

"There was. It's in the field beside the playground now." Aiden and Eddie both rush over to the windows while I turn to talk to Ruby, who restrains a smile.

"It's not funny. That room is disgusting. There's a pile of shit in the tub!"

Ruby bursts out laughing. "Too much for a waffle stomp?"

Mike and Max approach just as I ask, "What's a waffle stomp?"

Max chuckles and grabs the to-do list Ruby has left on the counter. He's still laughing as he makes his way back out the door.

"There will be no waffle stomping," Mike says, rolling his eyes. "The crime scene cleaners are coming."

"I want waffles!" Aiden pipes up. That does Ruby in, and

she retreats to the back office, red faced and vibrating with laughter.

"Go watch TV or something, Ade. I've got one more room and I'll be done."

He runs off, and I follow Ruby. "Are you going to live?" I ask, watching her wipe her eyes.

"Sorry, I didn't realize the boys were listening. Waffle stomp means to stomp a chunk of shit through the grating over the drain until it goes down."

Gross.

"I'll never get that image out of my head now. Thanks for that. All I have left is room 110, so I'll be right next door. Send Aiden over if he gets restless."

"Will do."

"Freaking waffle stomp," I grumble, and she dissolves into giggles again behind me.

The next room is thankfully normal, and less than thirty minutes later, Aiden and I are headed to Carl's Diner for lunch.

"Why couldn't we keep the goat?" Aiden whines as we take our seat in the red and white booth. "It's not fair."

"Life's not fair. And where would we keep it?"

"In my room. I could name him Eddie." Aiden shrugs out of his coat and slings it onto the seat beside him.

"Why would you call a goat Eddie?"

He shrugs. "He looks like he'd smell like Eddie."

Glenna, the waitress, chuckles at Aiden as she places a kid's menu in front of him.

"I want a grilled cheese and fries and a vanilla shake."

I raise my eyebrows at him, and he adds, "Please."

She takes my order as well. Just after she delivers our food, Aiden cries, "Neal! Mom, Neal's here!" He climbs up on his knees and waves his arms like everyone in the tiny diner didn't already hear him. "Neal! Come sit with us!"

Neal Chambers lives across the street from us and good god, he is wet dream material of the highest caliber. A strong, sculpted jawline, thick, wavy hair, and eyes the pale blue-green color of a robin's egg. He's a little over six feet tall, but that towers over my five foot six frame. Though he has an eleven year old daughter, he's only thirty-three, not at all too old for me if the situation was different. More than once I've had dreams about those lean muscles and flexing biceps.

I've done my best not to drool over him since he first introduced himself and helped us get settled into our new neighborhood. He is also a single parent, so we have that in common and often help each other out.

Neal slides into the booth beside Aiden. "Hey, buddy. Where are my fries?"

"You have to ask the lady." Aiden points to Glenna. "And say please and thank you, or Mom will give you the mean look."

Neal looks up at me with a smile I can feel in my stomach. "Are you giving the poor kid the mean look?"

"It's been a long morning. Someone locked a goat in one of the hotel bathrooms. Scared the crap out of me and then knocked me down."

Neal leans back, his smoky laugh filling the space. "And I thought having to sweep roaches out of a minivan was bad."

Neal manages a full-service car wash, and his horror stories rival mine. People are disgusting.

"Where's Bailey?" Aiden asks.

"She's at school. I'm just here to pick up my lunch, then I have to go back to work. Her hamster had babies yesterday, though. If you want to come over and see them tonight."

"Yes!" Aiden wiggles around in his seat. "Can I keep one?"

Neal gives me an apologetic look. "That's up to your mom."

"We'll see," I reply, taking a bite of my sandwich.

Aiden shrugs. "It's not as good as a maybe, but better than a no," he informs Neal. "She wouldn't let me have a goat today, but I could name a hamster Eddie."

Sighing, I restrain a laugh. "You are not naming any animal after that poor kid."

"But he smells."

"So does your butt."

Aiden laughs out loud and returns to his sandwich. Neal wears an ear to ear grin and shakes his head at me. I can only imagine how he sees me, arguing about hamsters and insulting my kid with stinky butt jokes.

Glenna brings Neal's boxed food over to the table, her eyes sweeping over him from head to toe. I can hardly blame her. He must get that everywhere he goes.

Getting to his feet, Neal says, "Bailey and I will be at the party a little early tomorrow to help you set up."

"Thank you. I'd really love the help."

"Be good, buddy," he tells Aiden, and I try not to stare as he walks away.

It's a massive failure. But with an ass like that, I'm not even close to sorry.

As promised, Neal and Bailey show up early to help me set up Aiden's fifth birthday party, and I couldn't be more grateful. I spent half the night baking cookies and his cake, wrapping his presents, and putting together gift bags. It's a bunch of dollar store crap the other kids' parents are sure to sneer at, but they can bite me. I've done what I can afford, and Aiden will love it.

Noble pulled some strings with his friends Cassidy and Wyatt, who own the community center, and they agreed to let us hold the party here. They even closed the pool to the public for three hours, so Aiden and his friends could swim.

I set up two folding tables in the corner, far away from the splash zone, one for the food and the other for the gift bags and presents. Because Aiden is a complete dinosaur fanatic, everything is dino themed. Noble even promised to have one of his buddies show up in a T-rex costume at some point. I can't wait to see the look on Aiden's face.

The only sore spot today came when Aiden asked if his grandmother was coming, and I had to tell him she couldn't make it. He shrugged it off quickly because they aren't close, but it was another reminder to me that I'm all my little boy has. My worst fear would be something happening to me because he'd end up in the foster system. I haven't heard good things.

Today, though, we're all about the happy shit. My little man is turning five.

The party is a success, judging by all the laughter coming from the kids. Two lifeguards watch over them as they play in the shallow end of the pool. It looks like half of Violent Circle is here. Emily—one of my friends from the circle—helps me plate up the pizzas that have just been delivered.

Neal approaches us, and he has changed into a pair of board shorts. "You aren't going to swim?" he asks.

Abs.

All I can see are clearly defined abs and the light sprinkling of chest hair that dissolves into a happy trail which definitely makes me happy.

An elbow catches me in my side and the oof sound that escapes is totally cool and feminine. I promise.

"Neal asked you a question," Emily says, amusement thick in her voice. The bitch has a pointy elbow, but I guess I should be thankful she made me stop ogling him.

"Sorry...I was watching the kids. What did you say?"

Neal's smirk makes it clear I'm busted, but he doesn't call me out. "You don't want to swim?"

"Oh, no, I can't. It's not exactly happy fun lady time in my pants right now."

The words spill out like someone else is saying them. What the hell is wrong with me? This is why I can't have nice things. Like normal boyfriends. Not that I'm interested in Neal. Still, I'd like to not be a weirdo who spouts random craziness.

"Okay then. Save me a piece," he says, nodding toward the pizza. He turns and strides toward the pool. At the last second, he takes a running jump and does a cannonball right in the center of the kids, making them all laugh and splash him.

"Smooth, girl," Emily laughs, and I scratch my nose with my middle finger. "I can't blame you though. Who knew superdad was so hot under those clothes?"

Aiden comes running up, water dripping down his face

from his hair. "Can I have some pizza now?"

"Dry off a little and grab a chair. Are you having fun?"

Denton chooses that moment to enter in the dino costume, and Aiden's body follows his head as it whips around so fast his feet slip out from under him. He seems to bounce off the floor, he gets up so fast, and cries, "Never mind! There's a T-rex!"

Denton stomps his way over to the pool, hitting the button that makes a roar sound from the costume, and the kids cheer, falling over each other to get out of the pool. Aiden runs up and stands in front of him.

"Happy birthday!" Denton roars, spreading the little T-rex arms. Aiden dives in for a hug, then runs around behind him and grabs the tail.

Denton has obviously never been around a group of five-year olds if he thinks this is going to go well. He's mobbed, poked, prodded, and hugged from every direction. He dances around, pretending to bite them and roaring until too many kids descend on him at once.

I'm sure they didn't mean for it to happen. They just pushed him off balance and the edge of the pool was right there. Emily gasps and grabs my arm as we watch for a long second that seems to go in slow motion. Denton teeters, and almost recovers before falling into the four-foot-deep water with an impressive splash.

I hear a yell of "Fappy!" from someone on the other side of the pool before laughter drowns out everything. Neal jumps in and helps Denton get to his feet, which isn't easy with the inflated costume floating around him.

A few of the kids look worried until Denton waves, then falls back and floats on his back, backstroking his way to the steps.

Emily looks at me, and we break into laughter. "Never a dull moment when the Frat Hell guys are involved."

The ear to ear smile on my little man's face could light a stadium.

"I wouldn't have it any other way."

Chapter Two

Neal

"Dad," Bailey moans. "I'm old enough to stay by myself."

"You're mature enough to stay by yourself, but the law says twelve, and I don't think orange is my color."

"Can I stay with Veronica?"

"She's working too."

Veronica and I have been spending more and more time together since Aiden's party a little over two months ago, always with the kids, since neither of us is looking for a relationship, no matter the rumors flying around the circle.

She rolls her eyes, slings her backpack over her shoulder and follows me to the car. I hate that I have to take her to work with me, but I'm lucky I can do so. It's only when I have to work a Saturday, and we have a comfortable lobby with wifi, so it's not like I'm torturing her. I've worked there since she was a baby, so she's practically grown up at Jetsky's Car Wash.

It's a bright, sunny day, and it looks like half the town is lined up at the entrance, though we don't open for a few minutes. We're experiencing a bit of an early Spring this year. It's over sixty degrees and everyone wants to get a winter's worth of salt and sludge off of their cars. It's going to be a long day.

Employees stand in clumps around the property, talking and laughing, and most wave at us as we make our way inside.

"Bails, it's going to be a busy day and I won't be in here much. You know where to find me." I hand her some money. "For snacks. Make sure you tell me or Beth that you're going." There's a small convenience store a couple blocks away where she likes to grab an ice cream if she gets bored.

"Thanks Dad."

"No problem, fam."

"Ugh." She stomps away, and I'm sure her eyes are in full roll mode.

What can I say? You have to find the little joys in life, like embarrassing your daughter with tween slang. It doesn't matter that I have no idea what half of the shit means.

Bailey and I have been on our own for over five years now, ever since her mother, Nina, ran away with some lowlife wanna-be musician. We haven't heard from her at all since Bailey was six. I know she's better off without her mother, but I also know that every birthday and holiday that passes without a card or phone call chips away more hope from my little girl.

She's grown up fast, and I couldn't ask for a better kid. She's responsible and mature, caring, and a good student. Everyone keeps telling me to beware the upcoming teen years, but so far, so good.

I stop to chat with Beth, the older lady who works the register. She's the only employee who has worked here longer than I have, and all the customers love her. "They're wrapped around the building already," I warn.

"I'm ready for them. You have Margo selling today, right? So it should go smoothly."

"Let's hope so." I turn around to say goodbye to Bailey, but she already has her nose in her tablet, and headphones on.

I do a quick walkthrough of the tunnel, making sure everything is as it should be, then give Margo a signal to open.

Jetsky's is a full-service car wash. Customers pull in and exit their vehicles, leaving us their car keys. There are two lanes, each with two employees who sweep out the cars first, then drive them around and put them on the track. Once they put them in neutral, they hop out, and the car is pulled through the automated wash and rinse. Two more employees catch it on the other side, and one drives it out before they both wash the windows and surfaces on the inside.

At the same time, two front line employees dry the vehicle and Armor-all the tires. The whole process takes less than ten minutes, but with bumper to bumper cars like today, there's no down time.

Fortunately, I'm a manager. I used to despise these types of days when I was sweeping or scrubbing windows, but now I oversee the employees, and chat up the customers, most of whom have been coming here for years. It's a good job, and the management position pays well enough that I don't struggle to give Bailey everything she needs and most of what she wants.

Living on Violent Circle, I'm sure most people assume I'm broke, and would be surprised that I have quite a bit of savings. No, I live in public housing because my bitch of an ex destroyed my credit, and you can't rent an apartment here with shitty credit. It sucks that I pay as much as others do to live in nicer apartments, but I like my neighbors, and everyone watches out for my daughter, so it's not all bad.

Besides, I have big plans in the works.

"Neal! How the hell are ya?" Harrison, the owner of a local car dealership grabs my hand and shakes it like a bottle of salad dressing. I swear I hear a knuckle crack—his or mine, I'm not sure which.

"Doing good. How about you?"

"Keeping my thumb on it. I noticed you're still driving that Nissan. I can get you in something a lot newer. We're overstocked so I can get you a hell of a deal."

Every single time.

Like clockwork, every week he brings in the vehicles, usually newly acquired from a rental company, for us to clean, and not a week goes by that he doesn't try to sell me a car.

"I'll be passing that car on to my daughter someday. It's a workhorse," I assure him.

We chat for a few minutes, and he heads inside to watch his cars make their way through the tunnel. I swear, the adults love to watch it through the floor to ceiling windows as much as kids do.

The morning goes by fast, and before I know it, Bailey hunts me down for lunch. I look up from speaking with a customer and she's waving my lunch box. I nod and gesture inside so I can finish the conversation, then head inside for a quick break.

"What did you make us?" I ask, handing her a soda and sitting beside her at the small breakroom table.

"Turkey and cheese sandwiches, baby carrots, and peaches."

She insisted on making our lunches this morning, and since I would've just ordered a pizza or grabbed hamburgers, I was happy for her to spare us the junk food. Sometimes I wonder who the adult is in our house.

We eat in silence for a few minutes before she asks, "Can we go to the zoo tomorrow? It's supposed to be warm and sunny again."

"That sounds like a great idea. We'll make a day of it."

"Can Veronica and Aiden come with us?"

"I don't see why not. If Veronica has to work, we can take Aiden."

"She doesn't."

My eyebrows jump up. "And how do you know that?"

"We chat on messenger."

I don't want to say anything to make Bailey feel bad or doubt herself, but I need to check she isn't pestering Veronica too much. I know she needs a woman to talk to, but it's also not her responsibility.

"Okay, I'll talk to her about it this evening."

"Thanks," she says with a grin.

"You know I'm on fleek, girl."

Soda spurts out her nose, and she coughs out a laugh. "You have no idea what that word means."

"It means I'm cool."

"If you say so."

Her smile brightens my day as it always does.

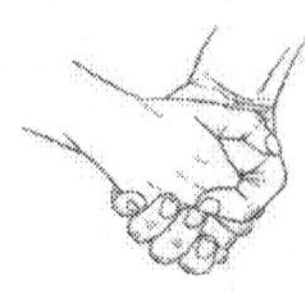

"Zip your jacket, Aiden," Veronica tells him as we make our way through the turnstiles at the entrance of the zoo.

"Why?"

"It's chilly."

"And the zookeepers won't mistake you for a monkey," I add.

He looks up at me and blinks. "Because monkeys don't wear jackets?"

"Exactly."

Aiden zips his jacket and Veronica shakes her head at me, grinning. "Where to first?"

"Lions!" Aiden cries.

"Snake house!" Bailey argues. Yeah, that's my kid. All these cute, fuzzy animals and she wants to see the creepiest one.

I must have a look on my face because Veronica gives me a teasing poke in the ribs. "Are you afraid of snakes?"

"You mean slithery, evil death ropes? It's not fear, it's common sense."

"My friend had a five-foot-long python she was getting rid of, but Dad wouldn't let me have it," Bailey adds.

"I saved our lives. And probably our neighbors. If it got loose, it could wipe us all out."

They laugh, and Aiden looks up at me. "I don't like snakes. I don't want to go in a snake's house."

"We'll let the girls go visit the snakes while we watch the lions."

Relief washes over Aiden's pinched face, and Veronica smiles as he takes my hand.

"Meet you in twenty minutes at the meerkat exhibit?" she suggests.

"Sounds good." I look down at Aiden who is wiggling around, but still holding my hand. "Ready, A?"

"Yes! I want to hear them roar!" He lets out a loud roar.

"Be good, Ade," Veronica warns, and she and Bailey head off in the opposite direction.

When we approach the lion enclosure, I'm glad to see they're out lying in the sun where we can see them. Aiden runs up to the glass and gives another loud roar, making the people around us laugh.

"They roar like dinosaurs! I saw it on TV." He peeks up at me, squinting. His brown hair has a red tint in the sunshine, a gift from his mother. "Are lions related to dinosaurs?"

"Sure they are. We're all related, if you go back in time far enough."

His jaw falls open. "I'm related to a dinosaur." The incredulity in his voice is hilarious. I've blown his mind.

"Sure, like, a third cousin, a thousand times removed."

Awe glows on his face as he watches a male lion approach a female who lies in a sunny patch of grass. The female doesn't appreciate his presence and jumps up, swatting at him. The male lets out a roar that rattles my teeth and makes Aiden slam his hands over his ears.

He wanted a roar, he got one.

"She got mad!" he exclaims, giggling.

The rejected male ambles over and lies right in front of us, his fur pressed against the glass. It's a photo opportunity if I've ever seen one. "Let's get your picture with the lion."

"'Kay."

Aiden sits cross legged on the ground, right in front of the lion, and I snap a couple of pictures. Just as I'm getting ready to tell him I'm done, the lion gets to its feet and snaps at the glass, trying to get at Aiden on the other side. I quickly switch to video, and a small crowd gathers as Aiden puts his hands to the glass, laughing as it tries to bite them.

"He wants to eat me!" His giggles mix in with the laughter of the crowd.

Aiden turns and smashes his butt against the glass, wiggling it back and forth, and the lion obliges, trying again to get a bite. I'm doing my best not to laugh too loud and ruin the video, but this kid is killing me. Bailey was such a calm, reasonable kid, even at this age. Boys are a different breed.

Finally, the lion loses interest, and walks away.

"That was awesome!" Aiden exclaims, taking my hand again as we head toward the meerkat exhibit. I can't wait to show Veronica the video.

Bailey and Veronica walk toward us, both wearing matching smiles as they talk. Since Veronica has been spending time with her, I've noticed Bailey has seemed more relaxed and happy. I do everything I can for her, but I think there are some things that just have to come from a woman.

"Mom! The lion tried to eat me! Did you know they're related to dinosaurs? And so am I! Neal knows because he went back in time!" Aiden rambles bouncing around his mother.

They crack up, and Veronica ruffles his hair. "That's great. Now we know why you snore like a T-Rex." She looks at me, her lip tucked in at the corner. "A time traveler, I had no idea."

Her red hair blows around her face, and I have to remind myself she's ten years younger than me. And that I'm not dating right now. "I don't tell everyone. It's top secret."

"I got to hold a python," Bailey tells me with a grin. "Did the lion really roar?"

"Yaaas, it was Gucci."

"Dad," she groans, but a snort of laughter sneaks through.

"What?" I put my arm around her as we walk. "You should've come with us, it was totally litty titty, fam jam."

"You have no idea what you're saying," she laughs.

"Mom says animals have titties. Girls have breasts," Aiden volunteers.

"I'll keep that in mind, buddy."

The meerkat exhibit is set up as a hands-on play experience. Glass tunnels wind around the enclosure and kids can crawl through them, getting a close view of the meerkats.

"Stay with Bailey!" Veronica calls to Aiden, as the kids run off to play, and we take a seat on a nearby bench where we can keep an eye on them. "I'm glad Bailey is here. I've had to drag my ass through the tunnels before. She's so good with him."

"She's always wanted a little brother. She'd take him home with us if she could."

Veronica sits back and takes a sip of her water before she says, "You don't have to tell me if you don't want to talk about it, but she mentioned she doesn't see her mother."

It's more unusual for a man to have sole custody of a daughter. I'm surprised it's taken her this long to ask. "It's okay. Her mom split when she was six. She hasn't seen or talked to her since."

"Same for Aiden's dad. I took him to court to have child support taken from his check, and he got visitation rights, but never uses them. Aiden knows who he is. He'll show up every once in a while and pretend to give a shit, but it doesn't last." She brushes an ant off her leg absently. "Aiden's better off."

"Were you married?" She's so young, just like I was when I had Bailey.

"No, he wanted to get married, but I didn't see the point. I don't ever plan to marry, anyway. We lived together at his mom's house, but when I got pregnant, they kicked me out. Accused me of trying to trap him." She rolls her eyes and huffs. "Because I'm after all that money he makes as a parking lot attendant. What about you? Divorced?"

"Yeah. We got married at twenty and had Bailey a little over a year later. I divorced her three years ago. Had to have a lawyer track her down to get the papers signed. As long as I agreed to no child support, she gave up full custody."

Veronica shakes her head. "I don't understand some people. No one could ever get Aiden away from me. You do a great job with Bailey. She's kind, and that's a rarity in girls that age."

"I appreciate you spending time with her. I think she was lonely for some female company."

"Same goes for Aiden. I know he's a handful, so you have to let me know when he's pestering you."

"That is one hilarious kid. So much personality."

A gorgeous smile lights up her face as she watches her son pop his head up from one of the holes in the tunnels. "It's been hard, but he's the best thing that's ever happened to me."

That smile makes me want things from her I have no right thinking about. She's ten years younger than me, and I can't have a real relationship right now even if I decided the age difference doesn't matter. She keeps her distance as well, and I can feel the invisible wall she's built around her.

She needs a friend, not another guy checking her out. God knows there are enough of them.

Chapter Three

Veronica

The day at the zoo was a wonderful idea and I think I had as much fun as the kids did. The hotel has been busy since the weather has gotten warm, and I've had to work all week, so when I clock out for my two days off, I breathe a sigh of relief.

Aiden waits for me at the edge of the playground. When he sees me approach, he yells "I'm out of here!" and shakes his ass at Eddie, who shakes a fist at him from the top of the slide.

"Dude, you have to stop shaking your butt at people," I tell him as we're getting in the car. "It's weird."

"Well, you said I can't tell him to kiss it."

I have to swallow back a chuckle. Fair point.

"Can we order a pizza tonight?"

"No, but we can make pizzas." Ordering in is a rarity reserved for special occasions. It's too damned expensive.

"Yay! I want sausage."

"We can do that."

"Can I have a soda? Can I stay up late tonight? And play video games?" Give the kid an inch and he'll hit you with the whole damn ruler.

He smiles at me in the rear-view mirror. "You can have a root beer with dinner and then play your game. Bedtime is the same. Nice try, though."

He shrugs. "I had to try. You always tell me to try."

He's got me there.

If we're having pizza, then a stop at the grocery store is necessary. It's not crowded so I hope to get in and out quickly since I'm filthy from work and probably look like a homeless person. It never works out that way though, does it? If you dress up and your makeup and hair are perfect, you won't see anyone. Leave the house in pajama bottoms with your hair in a struggle bun and it's high school reunion time in the produce department.

Aiden grabs a kiddie cart and follows me down an aisle to grab his root beer. I don't let him have soda very often, but at least root beer is caffeine free. We manage to grab all the ingredients for our pizza and I'm almost to the cashier when I hear a laugh I could go my whole life without hearing again.

Aiden's father, Clint, stands a few feet away, digging through a bin of candy bars, a thin blond girl at his side. Aiden is oblivious, and I really don't want this to turn into an ugly confrontation in a grocery store.

"Here, why don't you go play the claw machine," I tell Aiden, handing him some quarters. "Stay right there where I can see you."

"Thanks!" He runs off to the machine, in the opposite direction of his father, who has now noticed us.

He does exactly what I expect him to do, which is why I didn't want Aiden to see him. He sneers at me, grabs the girl's hand, and gets in the line farthest away from me. After he checks out, he walks right past his son, just a few inches behind him, moving like his heels are on fire so Aiden won't see him. Because what could be worse than having to say hi to your kid?

Fucking waste of space.

Worthless piece of shit.

There's no anger in this world like the anger you feel when someone hurts your kid or does them wrong. Every time I see him, my hatred grows. I have to remind myself that Aiden is better off without people like that in his life.

I manage to swallow down the rage and plaster on a smile for my son as he rushes up to me carrying a stuffed dog. "I won!"

"That's great!" I hug him. "You're getting good at that machine. What are you going to name it?"

Aiden rattles on as I put the groceries in the car, but I don't hear much. Poor kid is placated with a few uh-huhs and yeahs while I chew on my anger and try to shake it off. It's been nearly a year since I've seen Clint. He stopped by and promised to return that evening to take Aiden to the park. Of course, he didn't, and watching my little boy stand in the door for over two hours waiting for him tore pieces out of me.

All I can think is the horrible stuff I'd wish on him.

Like a bout of uncontrollable diarrhea combined with a prolapsed anus. I flipped through a medical book once and found a picture of a prolapsed anus that gives me nightmares to this day. Who knew your asshole could just decide to jump out of your body? Horrific. And perfect for him.

When we get home, Aiden makes a beeline for his video game, and I take a quick shower while he's occupied. Since I'm usually kind of strict when it comes to screen time, I know he'll be glued to it until I pry him away. It's late, and I have no intention of going anywhere else tonight, so I throw on some leggings and a long shirt, then put my hair up in a messy bun when it's only about half dry. I'll regret it later when I have to work out a bunch of knots, but I'm tired and all I want to do is get dinner ready then relax with a book.

After I fry the sausage and chop up some green peppers for my side of the pizza, I yell for Aiden. He loves to put the toppings on.

"Coming!" He runs into the room and jerks out the chair, making me wince at the horrible scraping sound. "I'm on level five!"

"Yeah? What's your record?"

"Level ten. I'm going to beat it tonight."

He grins at me, and I notice he's wiggling a tooth with his tongue. "Do you have a loose tooth?"

"Yeah, it won't come out though."

"Let me see."

The tooth barely moves when I touch it. "It's not ready.

Don't worry. It'll fall out in its own time."

"Then I can take it to the park and gross out the twins."

The poor twin girls who visit their mother here on weekends are his intended victims. They're his age, and they probably wouldn't tease him so much if he didn't take every chance to tell them they aren't as cool as Bailey.

"Don't be mean."

He raises an eyebrow at me, and I swallow back a laugh. "They tried to put lipstick on me last week."

"What did you do?"

"Ran. And Bailey made them stop."

Bailey to the rescue.

With me overseeing him, Aiden spreads the sauce, sprinkles on the cheese and sausage, and then hops off his chair. "You can do the yucky green stuff."

"Wash your hands before you touch the controller!" I call, as he sprints back toward the living room.

The sound of running water from the bathroom tells me I caught him in time. While the pizza cooks, I actually have a few minutes to sit at the table and read a chapter of the horror book one of the neighbors loaned me. It's really getting good. I see how I'm going to be spending my night.

After the pizza is cool, Aiden wolfs down two slices and goes back to his game. Yeah, I'm going to be that terrible parent tonight. He can play until it's time for a bath and bed.

"You can play until nine. Then bath and bed, kiddo. You hear me?"

He nods, his eyes never leaving the screen.

My phone beeps with a text from Neal.

Neal: Can you come over? I have a bit of an emergency.

Neal has never asked me for help. I hope Bailey is okay.

I can see Mallory sitting on her front step, so I stick my head out my door. "Mallory? Do you think you could come and sit with Aiden for just a few minutes? I'm just going across the street to Neal's."

She gives me a knowing grin and pulls her front door shut. “Sure. Take your time. I got nothing going on tonight.”

She follows me into my living room. “Aiden, Mallory is going to stay with you for a few minutes while I go across the street.”

He doesn’t look up. “’Kay.”

“He’s in video game land so it’ll be like babysitting a plant. I’ll be right back. Help yourself to some pizza if you want. It’s on the stove.”

Mallory takes a seat on the couch, and I rush out the door.

Neal meets me at his door, looking harried, and ushers me inside. “What’s going on?”

Bailey sits on the couch. She looks miserable and a bit pale. “Dad wants to take me to the hospital!”

“What’s wrong?” I turn to regard Neal, and he runs a hand across his face, his palm rasping against his five o’clock shadow.

“I didn’t know what else to do. I tried to reach my sister, but she’s not answering, and she’d probably tell her to wear a fig leaf and do a rain dance or some shit.” He’s rambling on, and I still have no idea what the problem is.

“Bailey, are you feeling sick?”

Her cheeks color, and she looks at her feet as she mumbles, “I’m bleeding.”

Bleeding? I don’t see any blood. Then it hits me.

Surely not. He is not freaking out and threatening to take her to a hospital for that.

“Did you get your period?” I ask, softening my voice and sitting beside her.

She nods, still staring at her feet, and a tear drops to her lap. “I don’t need a hospital for that, do I?”

“No, honey.” A snort jumps out, and I cover my mouth.

She gives me a bemused look. “I’m sorry. I’m laughing at your dad, not you. He’s completely lost it.”

A tentative smile crawls across her face. “Yeah, he has.”

“How do you feel?” I ask, brushing her hair back.

“My stomach hurts. Other than that, okay I guess.”

“I’m going to run home and grab you a pad, then we’ll go

shopping for the stuff you need, okay? Everything is going to be all right. I know it's scary when you see the blood for the first time, and it's okay to be afraid, but it's not as bad as you think."

It's a week of hell where your baby box declares war and takes no prisoners, but she'll find that out in her own time.

She hugs me, and I wrap my arms around her. "It sucks in a lot of ways, but it also means you're growing up. Joining the exclusive club that's for women only. That's something to celebrate, and tradition insists we do it with chocolate."

She smiles, and I whisper. "Look at your dad. I think you broke him."

Giggles spill out of her as we stare at Neal, who is frozen in place, watching us like we might explode.

"Neal, relax. She's fine. If you want to go stay with Aiden, we'll go to the supercenter and get her taken care of."

"Thank you," he breathes.

I make a quick trip home and back to bring her a pad. "Just peel the back off and stick it on your panties. The wings wrap around the edges to keep it in place."

"Do I have time to take a quick shower? It's kind of...everywhere."

"Sure. Take your time, hun. And if you rinse the clothes with cold water, the blood will probably come out."

I leave her to get cleaned up and find Neal pacing the living room. His eyes are wide when he looks up at me. "I'm not ready for this. She's my baby girl."

He is fucking adorable right now.

"Yes, but she's not a baby. Were you really going to take her to the hospital?"

He shrugs, a sheepish smile in place. "I figured they could handle it."

"It's a period. You aren't disarming a bomb. And what the hell was that about a rain dance?"

He bursts out laughing. "You haven't met my sister yet. She's into all that holistic, homeopathic stuff. She would've had me giving her wheat germ supplements to grow more blood or some shit."

He takes a seat across from me. "Seriously, tell me what I need to do to make this easier for her."

"Just be understanding when she's moody or acting out. Periods are hard enough when you're grown. During puberty, it's brutal. Let her be angry or cry or laugh or do all three at the same time and don't look for a logical explanation because it's all hormones."

"Puberty, fuck. I thought I had until thirteen at least."

"Girls mature faster. I started at eleven, so I know how she feels. I'll take her to get what she needs. Do you have any painkillers?"

"Tylenol."

"I'll get her some Naproxen. It works better for cramps."

We hear the shower shut off. "Expect some stained sheets and clothes. If you use a stain blocker stick and wash them on cold, most will come clean."

He nods and smiles at her as she walks in, her wet hair pulled into a ponytail. She's wearing a pair of sweat pants and a hoodie. "You've nailed the uterus uniform," I tell her. "Leggings are good too."

She gives us a reluctant smile. "I'm ready."

Neal hugs her and kisses the top of her head. "Sorry I freaked out."

"It's okay."

Neal locks his door, and we head to my place. Mallory sits on the couch watching Aiden play his game.

"Thanks Mallory. I really appreciate you keeping an eye on him," I tell her. "Neal is going to sit with him while we run an errand."

"Sure, anytime. I should get going. I have company coming."

"Neal! Play the second player!" Aiden pipes up, shoving the controller toward him. He's suddenly aware a world still exists outside his game.

"You'll have to teach me," Neal tells him, sitting cross legged on the floor beside him.

"You have until I get back, Aiden. Then it's bath and bed."

Aiden doesn't answer, and Neal waves us off.

Bailey is quiet until we get to the store. "I don't want tampons," she whispers.

"There are a lot of different pads, and they're really thin. We'll get a couple of different brands, so you can see what works for you."

We end up with everything I can think of to help during the monthly egg massacre. Pads, painkillers, a heating pad, a chocolate cake, and some plain colored cotton panties. "You'll end up sacrificing a pair every now and then. It happens to all of us. Better to have some extras," I tell her.

I also pick up a small calendar and show her how to count the days, so she can try to figure out her cycle. "It may not be regular when you're so young, so don't be surprised if it doesn't stick to a schedule at first. Mine didn't."

"God, it's going to be every month," she groans as we climb back into my car. "I wish I was a boy."

"Nah, can you imagine how annoying having a penis and testicles must be?"

She giggles. "That's true. They must get in the way. I wonder if they ever sit on them."

"That's a question I'd pay to hear you ask your dad," I laugh.

"I think I traumatized him enough for one night." She hesitates for a second before asking, "Can I stay with you tonight?"

My heart goes out to her, and I understand wanting a woman she trusts close by. "Absolutely. But you have to share the chocolate cake."

"Deal."

Aiden is practically falling asleep sitting in front of the TV when we walk in. "Aiden, it's bed time. You can just take a bath in the morning."

I'll have to wash his sheets, but it's about time anyway.

"'Kay."

I know he's tired when he doesn't argue. I glance at Neal. "Hang out while I get him to bed, okay?"

"Yeah."

Aiden is asleep before I shut his bedroom door. I grab a pillow and blanket from my bed, then plug in the heating pad beside it before returning to the living room.

Bailey is curled up in the corner of the couch, her eyes drooping. "Do you want a piece of cake?"

"Not right now. Dad said I can stay the night."

He'd probably be happy for her to stay three to five days. "Come on. You can have my bed. I sleep on the couch half the time."

She climbs into bed, and I bring her a glass of water and a painkiller. "If you wake up hurting, put the heating pad on your stomach, but keep it on low. And come get me if you need me."

"I will. Thanks, Veronica." She snuggles down under the covers.

"You're welcome, honey. Things will look better in the morning." I turn off the bedside lamp.

"And we can have cake for breakfast," she murmurs.

"It's a plan."

I close the bedroom door and return to the living room where Neal waits. "Do you need another pep talk too?" I tease.

He gathers the two video game controllers from the floor and places them on the coffee table. "I'm not going to live down tonight, am I?"

"No way."

Taking a seat on the couch, he flashes me a smile that makes me want to take my panties off. "Thanks for everything you did for her."

"Anytime. She's such a sweet kid, and she'll be fine. This is all normal stuff, you know?"

He chuckles, and his head falls back on the top of the couch. "Yeah, well, I'm more qualified to discuss hard-ons and shaving."

Exhaustion is catching up with me as I flop onto the opposite side of the couch. "Don't worry, she'll have those questions too."

"Now you're just torturing me."

"Maybe a little." I fold my legs underneath me. "I was glad

for the distraction tonight. I ran into Aiden's father at the grocery store."

Neal's brow crumples. "What happened?"

"He ignored me, sneaked past Aiden, and took off. Not that I wanted him to say anything to him, but—"

"But he should want to," Neal finishes. Even his mad face is adorable. His lips press together, and a line appears in the center of his forehead. "He'd better hope I never run into him. Aiden's a great kid. He should be proud."

"I know. There's no use thinking about it though, so I just wish terrible things on him in my head."

His eyebrow raises. "Like car accidents and stuff?"

"No, more like, I hope his asshole grows taste buds."

The sound of his laughter does things to me. It's deep and quiet, fading to almost silent when he laughs really hard, his body vibrating. His pale blue eyes glow in the low light when he looks at me.

"I hope I never piss you off. Okay, let's come up with some more bad luck for…"

"Clint."

"Clit? You actually got naked for a guy named Clit?"

"Clint!" I repeat, shoving him. "He wouldn't know a clit if it slapped him in the face. I hope he gets that feeling that he needs to sneeze, but can never sneeze."

Neal sits back and crosses his arms, thinking. "I hope every time he has to shit, there's one stubborn chunk that gets stuck. So no matter how long he wipes, it's like wiping the tip of a marker."

"Ew! That's gross." The stress of the day lifts from my shoulders as I laugh. "I hope the sound is just slightly out of sync on every video he ever tries to watch."

"Diabolical. I hope every pizza he orders is delivered upside down."

"Oh, heartless. Pizza is life." He smiles at me, and I swear it goes straight to my stomach. What the hell, Veronica? You know he's off limits.

"Feel better?"

"I do. Now move your ass so I can crash. It's been a long

day."

"Yes, dear," he mocks, getting to his feet.

I'm grabbed in an unexpected hug when I stand. His body is so warm, and he smells amazing. My muscles relax, and I squeeze him back. When he lets go, he steps back and awkwardness sneaks in around us. "Good night," he finally says.

"Good night."

As tired as I am, I spend a few minutes tossing and turning, my unsettled emotions taking over. I can't pinpoint what I'm feeling. Maybe I'm just freaking out because I'm feeling something for a man when I haven't let that happen for a long time.

I need to put things in perspective again.

Neal is just a friend. I'm not looking for a relationship or a hookup even if he was willing. I have enough to worry about just keeping a roof over my son's head. There's just not room for anyone else.

Chapter Four

Neal

"Dad!" Bailey runs into the house, her ponytail flying. "Veronica got an eviction letter and so did the twin's mom!"

What the hell?

My hands fall to her shoulders as she looks up at me. "What are you talking about?"

"They put letters on their door that say they could get kicked out. Everyone is talking about it."

This may be a close-knit neighborhood, but that doesn't include the management. Since they've taken over, it's one new draconian rule after another. The show we put on during the monthly inspections put a stop to those at least. I think Noble masturbating to gay porn probably made the decision there, but it hasn't stopped them from trying more and more bullshit.

George, the owner of Jetsky's Car Wash, set me up with a lawyer who does pro bono work for low income people, and he's working on gathering evidence of some of the clearly illegal practices. Like stealing the kids toys and bikes if they're left in the yard. And I don't mean they pick up toys left out for days. A mother of a two-year-old took him in to change a diaper and came back to find his little ride-on toy gone. When she called the office, they told her she could buy it back for five dollars. We live in the poorest neighborhood in town and they're stealing from kids who have little to nothing.

"Is Veronica home?" I ask Bailey.

"She's over at the park talking to the twins' mom."

I've seen Veronica almost every day since our zoo trip, but I still feel the same anticipation when I head out the door.

A group of neighbors mill around the park, standing in small groups and sitting at the picnic table while their kids play.

Veronica walks toward me as I approach, her jaw tight and rage in her eyes. I've never seen her so pissed off. "What's going on?"

Without a word, she hands me a sheet of paper. "I got another threat letter."

Threat letters, as we've started calling them, have become a common thing. They leave a letter on everyone's door when they change a rule or notice something they don't like. Last week a man on the other end got one because he had his granddaughter visiting, and she drew a hopscotch on the sidewalk with chalk. They threatened him with eviction if it happened again. Then they put a letter on the rest of the doors stating that sidewalk chalk is graffiti and grounds for eviction. You can't make this shit up.

They can't just say not to do something, it always includes an *or else* eviction threat. It seems they get off on threatening to make poor people homeless. One bit of advice I have received from the lawyer is that none of the reasons they've given would justify an eviction, and to save the letters.

Veronica's letter is infuriating and it's everything I can do not to go down to the office, drag the bastards outside, and show them how you should treat a bully.

My teeth grind as I read the main paragraph again.

Your son has been seen throwing handfuls of the rubber mulch into the air in the playground. Rubber mulch is very expensive and if he persists in this behavior, you will be charged for the replacement mulch and face eviction. Please remedy this situation.

An eviction threat for a kid playing in the playground.

Veronica's smile is bitter when I look up at her, and she turns to glance back at her son who is playing with some other kids in the playground. "I asked Aiden and the other kids if they threw the mulch, and they said they were tossing it up in the air and letting it rain down on them. It's fucking ridiculous. They weren't taking it out of the park or harming anything."

Jani speaks up. "And even if it is something they don't want the kids doing, how hard is it to say, hey, don't play with the mulch. There, problem solved. No, they have to be a dick sneeze about it and threaten people."

Aiden runs up, and his gaze travels around the circle of adults before he asks, "Am I in trouble?"

Veronica smooths her hand over his hair. "Not at all. Just don't throw the mulch and tell the other kids the same thing, okay?"

"Okay. Damon says his aunt almost got kicked out because he jumped the fence last week, so don't jump fences," he warns the group with a wise nod.

Noble grins at him. "No fence jumping. Got it, dude." When Aiden runs off, Noble turns to me. "Yeah, there's more to that story. They didn't just tag her door. Freida saw the kid jump the fence and asked him if he wanted to make his aunt homeless because if he did it again, she'd be out. He's nine."

Nodding, I announce. "If you all can bring me copies of the threat letters you've received, I'll get them to the lawyer. Also, any written statements you might be willing to contribute about the way you or your kids have been treated. None of this shit is legal." I look around at everyone. "And I understand if that's not a risk you're willing to take as well. We all have to keep a roof over our heads."

So many here can't afford to move, which is why I decided to lead this cause. I'm close to having my credit repaired and I can move if I have to. It would suck, because I have a few goals in mind I'm trying to reach to make sure we're good and stable first, but it could be done. If they're going to retaliate by evicting someone, better it be us than a family that would end up on the street.

"I have a copier if anyone needs to use it," Noble volunteers before pulling me aside. "I have an idea. You know I work at WFUK, and if I brought this to their attention, they may be willing to do a story. Take this shit public. I wanted to see what the lawyer thought about that idea first, though."

"I'll get in touch with him this week and see if he thinks it's a good idea."

Noble nods, then grins at me. "By the way, we need a DM for Dungeons and Dragons tonight. You said you used to play when you were young."

"You mean when this was all still farm land?" I scoff. "I'm thirty-three, not eighty."

"Whatever, just grab your daily fiber drink, and come and DM for us."

It's been years since I played D&D, and the nerd in me is still strong. Noble and his friends might be a bunch of college kids, but they're fun to be around, at least in small doses. I guess that's the old man in me talking. It's funny I don't see Veronica the same way. "What time?"

"Eight o'clock."

"I'll be there."

Noble only lives a few doors down, so I'm fine with letting Bailey stay alone for a couple of hours, and she'll be thrilled.

Noble goes back to the group, and I start back across the street to my apartment to let Bailey know that no one is being evicted. It pisses me off that the management makes these kids worry over things that are in no way a child's problem.

"Neal!" Veronica calls, and jogs to catch up with me. Wow, she's not wearing a bra. "Did you hear about the lock-in at the community center this weekend?"

"What's a lock-in?"

She falls in step beside me. "Since it's spring break, they're having a little sleepover party for kids ages four and up. They'll have activities for them and they'll camp out in the gym in their sleeping bags. I guess I'm going to let Aiden go since he's begging to, and I thought Bailey might be interested."

"I'm sure she will. Thanks for letting me know." I pause, laying my hand on her arm. "Don't worry about these threat letters. Nobody is getting evicted. I've got this."

A smile stretches across her cheeks. "I believe you." She

glances back at Aiden who is sitting on the curb. "I'd better get back to Aiden. He's driving me nuts. He won't eat because he has a loose tooth, but he's afraid to let me pull it. I swear, I'm going to pull it while he's asleep."

"Bailey was the same way. Can I try something?"

"Sure, but I doubt he'll go for it."

"I'll be over in just a minute."

They head back to her apartment, and I run inside to grab a remote-controlled airplane. It was a gift to Bailey, but I've played with it more. Bailey was all freaked out over pulling a loose tooth, and I found it was best to find a creative way to do it and get her involved. Last time we tied one to a nerf dart and had her shoot the gun. Aiden likes planes so this should work well.

"A, come check this out!" I call to him as I step into Veronica's yard.

He rushes over. "A plane! Can I fly it?"

"You sure can, but this is a special plane. It goes faster if you give it some special fuel." Veronica watches us, and I give her a wink.

"Like gas?"

"Well, your mom says you have a loose tooth." I produce a roll of floss and show him. "If I put this string around your tooth, the plane will go extra fast, and the tooth will fall out without you even feeling it."

His mouth drops open and he whispers, "Really?"

Bailey speaks up, showing him where one of her back teeth is missing. "It worked with mine."

"Okay! Do mine! I want to make the plane fly fast!"

Aiden holds still as I tie the floss around the tooth. It damn near comes out just with that, so this will be easy. "Okay, let's do it." I turn the plane on and show him how to control it. I made the floss long enough to give it enough slack that the tooth won't catch until the plane is in the air and a few feet away. "You can take off anytime, Captain."

Grinning with excitement, he presses the lever forward and the plane darts into the air, taking his tooth with it in a split second. "It does go fast!" he exclaims.

"Let me show you how to turn it around." We spend a few minutes guiding the plane around the yard before he lands it on the sidewalk.

"That was so cool! When will my tooth fall out?"

Bailey laughs and follows the floss until she picks up the tooth lying at the end. "Your tooth is right here."

Aiden's stunned look makes us all laugh especially when he puts his fingers in his mouth and feels the hole. "It worked! Mom, look! It didn't hurt!" he cries, running over to show her the gap.

Veronica hugs him and beams at me. "It did! What do you tell Neal?"

"Thank you!" he shouts and runs over, hugging my leg.

Bailey sits down with him to look at his tooth while I chat with Veronica for another minute until she says, "Thanks again. I have to go into work for a few hours since the front desk clerk is sick. We'll see you later."

And now I need to brush the dust off of my D&D handbook and drag out one of my old stories for tonight.

I'm officially too old to hang out with college kids. Not that I wasn't aware of that fact, but his offer for a Dungeons and Dragons game had me all nostalgic for the days when I played in high school and college.

Some things you can't go back to.

My memories of Dungeons and Dragons were late nights spent creating these layered, deeply thought out worlds, full of magic and mystery. We designed characters that had personalities, strengths, weaknesses, and personal goals.

Some defining moments from the night with Noble and the Frat Hell guys were when Kenny insisted his character was still armed because he had an arrow hidden up his ass, and when another proclaimed his penis a weapon. They then had to roll the dice for dick size. Length and girth. Since he rolled a two, followed by a ten, that's what he was stuck with.

They named it the cheese wheel.

Don't get me wrong, it was hilarious and fun. Just not the same. I think I'll stick to my poker nights and bowling league.

Chapter Five

Veronica

"Don't forget my pillow!" Aiden calls, dancing around with his backpack slapping against his back.

"It's inside the sleeping bag," I remind him, putting everything in the trunk.

"I'm going to have the coolest sleeping bag there!"

"No one else will have anything like it," I laugh. Yeah, that would be because my kid had a heart attack when he saw a Five Finger Death Punch sleeping bag online, and instantly added it to his Christmas list last November. I can already hear the judgmental *Hmms* being uttered by the soccer moms when they see the heavy metal band bag spread out amongst all the Spiderman and cartoon characters. I can't give a shit, though. He loves it, slept in it for a week after he got it, and that's all that matters to me.

The Spring Break Lock In seems to be popular, judging by all the cars crammed into the parking lot of the community center. I wasn't sure about this whole thing at first. Aiden is only five, and he's never spent a night without me, but Neal assured me the people who are holding this party are responsible and trustworthy. Wyatt and his wife, Cassidy, are known and well liked on the Circle, since Cassidy used to live in what's now my apartment.

A parking spot opens up when a minivan carrying two smiling parents backs out. A kid free night during the spring break holiday? People couldn't sign up fast enough, and I'm betting the liquor stores are doing extra business tonight, along with the condom industry.

Aiden squirms with excitement, dancing around me while I unload the trunk. "Stay with me until we figure out where you're supposed to go, Ade."

We make our way inside, and Bailey rushes up to hug me. "Hey, the little kids are in the gym with Miss Cassidy and Noble."

Aiden slams his hands to his hips. "I ain't little! I just turned five."

Bailey grins at the offense in his tone. "Shoot. They have a bounce house in the gym. I guess you're too old for that, huh?"

Aiden's ears seem to stand up. "A bounce house?" He jerks his gaze up to me. "Can I?"

"Go for it."

He's off with Bailey in a flash, leaving me smiling after him. I'm glad I'm the only one stressing over being apart for a night.

About fifteen kids, ranging in age from five to eight, run around the large gymnasium, climbing in and out of a bouncy castle, and chasing one another.

"Hey Veronica!" Noble approaches with a pretty brunette. "I don't think you've met Cassidy, have you?"

"I haven't." Cassidy shakes my hand, and I add. "It's nice to meet you. Everyone says good things about you on the Circle." Then I realize how that must've sounded. "Not that everyone talks about you. It's not like gossip or anything. I just live in your old apartment, so it's bound to come up and—" I stop myself. I'm babbling like an idiot. "I'm going to stop now."

Cassidy laughs and glances at Noble, then back to me. "You're going to fit right in here." She nods toward Aiden who is approaching us with pursed lips. "This is your boy?"

"Yes." I lay my hand on his shoulder when he reaches me. "This is Aiden, Aiden, this is Ms. Cassidy." I heard the other children addressing her that way, so that's what I'm going with.

Cassidy kneels to speak with him. "I'm glad you came, Aiden. We're going to have a good time tonight. And if you need anything, you just come and find me or Noble, okay?"

"Okay." He grins. "I like Noble. He's funny."

Cassidy grins at me. "Noble is a big kid. They all love him."

"Mom?" Aiden says, tugging the hem of my shirt. "Eddie is here."

Cassidy turns to speak to another parent, so I pull Aiden aside. "He is?"

"Yeah, and he tried to say he's still my boss, and I can't go in the bounce house unless he says."

Not this again. "Is he your boss?"

"No!"

"Then why are you listening to him?"

Aiden's face scrunches in thought. "I don't know."

"Just ignore it, Ade."

Noble overhears the conversation and steps in. "If you have any problems, you come and tell me, okay? Everyone gets to play in the bounce house. We're going to have fun."

A smile darts across Aiden's face. "Okay." He runs and dives back inside the bouncy castle.

"Just put his sleeping bag and backpack in that corner," Noble says.

After following his direction, I just kind of stand there, fidgeting. It feels so strange to just...leave my kid somewhere. "If he wants to come home or anything..."

"I've got your phone number. I'll call you," Noble assures me.

"I know that look," Neal says, joining us. "First time he's spent a night away from home?"

"Is it that obvious?"

Neal chuckles and nods toward the door. "You need a drink. Why don't I stop at the liquor store and I'll remind you what a night away from kids feels like? You never know when you'll get another one."

"Sounds good." Going back to my empty apartment so I can worry over Aiden every second isn't going to do me any good. I can't believe I'm reacting this way. I've never been particularly overprotective. I don't stop him from doing things where he may get hurt, or baby him when he's made a mistake and needs to apologize. Why am I losing it over one night away from him when he's in perfectly capable hands?

"I'll just tell him I'm leaving."

Neal and Noble accompany me over to the bounce house, and we look through the mesh at the mess of jumping, giggling children. Two voices stand out over the rest, and of course, one is my son.

"You can't jump over there! It's against my rules!" Eddie shouts. I can't blame Aiden for how he feels about him. As sorry as I feel for the kid, he does behave like a little d-bag.

Noble opens his mouth to intervene, but Aiden beats him to it.

"I can do what I want. You're just mad cause you got Zacktly Disease."

"What's Zacktly Disease?" a little girl asks, struggling to stay on her feet.

Aiden faces Eddie with a grin. "Your face looks zacktly like your butt!"

All the kids laugh, and the little girl looks at Aiden like he's the best thing she's ever seen.

"Aiden!" I call out, and he runs over, slamming his hands into the mesh, a look of joy on his face. I'm not even going to say anything. I mean, really? How much abuse is he supposed to take from the kid? I taught him to use his words, not his fists. It's not my fault he's so damned good at it.

"I'm going to go now. You listen to Noble and Cassidy, and have fun."

"I will! Bye!" He rushes off without a backward glance. A few seconds later, fingers wrap around my arm and Neal's amused voice fills my ear.

"Come on. He's fine. Time to go."

Nodding, I glance at Noble. "Good luck. You're a saint."

When I make the turn into our apartment complex, a laugh erupts from my throat. The playground and the picnic table are covered in people. You can't give Violent Circle a night with no kids. We don't know how to act. In other words, this is going to be fun.

Denton waves at me and calls my name as I get out of my car. Before I can answer, all the guys from Frat Hell echo him in unison. They're a crazy bunch of college guys and everyone likes them. "Get your ass over here!" Denton calls. "We picked up a keg!"

They did. A metal tub of ice has pride of place in the center of the basketball court, a silver keg resting inside.

"Spring break, baby!" Kenny yells, chugging a beer faster than I thought humanly possible.

It hadn't occurred to me that the college kids were on break as well. Looking around, there are plenty of neighbors out here who will have to drag their hungover asses to work tomorrow. From teenagers to a few of the elderly people who live on the opposite end of the circle, everyone is out and having fun. I'm glad my days off work happened to coincide.

Neal parks his car across the street at his place, then meets me as I'm walking to my door. "We should've seen this coming," he laughs.

"Is this a normal Spring break thing?"

"No, but if the community center makes the lock-in an annual thing, I'm sure this will be too."

He follows me inside as I unlock my door. A loud bout of laughter echoes outside, and we look at each other. "You want to?"

"Yep," I agree, switching to my comfortable sneakers. "You know something crazy is going to happen."

Neal peeks out the window. "Uh…Barney just rolled down the spiral slide."

A snort leaps out of me. "Rolled?"

"Well, it wasn't a smooth journey, I can tell you that."

"Normal Friday for him." Barney's name is actually Barry,

and he's our resident drunk, nicknamed after the Simpsons character. Everyone watches out for him, makes sure he gets home, tries to keep him from getting arrested or hurt. He's dead set against rehab so it's pretty much all anyone can do.

"Ready, V?"

My heart stutters a little at the nickname, something he's never called me before. It's silly, I know. He calls Aiden "A". It doesn't mean anything, but it doesn't escape my notice either.

"As I'll ever be."

We start toward the park together, and Samantha, my neighbor from two doors down, falls in step with us. I don't know her well, but she's always been nice to me. The consensus around the Circle is that her legs open more than a refrigerator, but no one really cares or judges. We all have our shit to deal with.

"Hi Veronica." Before I can reply, she's talking to Neal.

"Neal Chambers, you just get better looking every time I see you."

Neal grins down at her. "It's good to see you too."

Her lips purse a bit at his diplomatic answer, then thin into a knowing smile when she looks at me. I have no doubt she'll be feeding the rumors of mine and Neal's nonexistent, but nevertheless torrid love affair.

There are a lot of things I like about our neighbors. Despite it being a poor area where everyone is struggling to get by, they all look out for each other. The downside is you can't fart without someone racing away to tell the next person how it smelled and sounded. Being the new girl here has been an adjustment, but I think I fit in pretty well.

Samantha heads over to the group of people sitting in the park, and we make our way over to the keg. The ubiquitous red solo cups are piled beside it, but we detour around it since we have our own bottles.

We take a seat at the picnic table, along with a few others and watch as a pickup game forms on the basketball court. "It's getting dark," I comment. "No way they're going to be able to see the basket."

"Looks like they have that covered," Neal replies with a

chuckle, gesturing to Kenny and Trey, who approach with matching cheesy smiles. They each have a portable spotlight in their hands and a ton of extension cord.

"Where the hell are you going to plug that in, you idgits?"

My mouth falls open in shock when I see who asked the question. One of the few neighbors I haven't met is Darla. She's over sixty if I had to guess, and probably one of the stranger people I've seen here. Every day Darla walks down the circle, passing in front of my apartment, before crossing the street to a small grocery store. That's not odd in and of itself, but she always wears the same thing: a black, wide brim, floppy sun hat and a tan, calf length trench coat.

I've never seen her in anything else. When I commented on it to Noble once, he chuckled and said, "It doesn't matter if it's ten degrees or a hundred, she wears that coat and hat. Just watching her walk down the street like that when the temp is over a hundred and the humidity is sky high makes me sweat."

He didn't have an explanation, but he did tell me it does no good to offer her a ride. She always refuses.

Trey gives her a wide smile. "We'll figure it out, Ms. Darla, just you wait."

"Do you want a beer?" Neal asks her.

"Of course I do. I was waiting to see who'd be a gentleman and ask."

As he fills up her cup, I introduce myself. "Hi, I'm Veronica. I moved into 207 a few months ago."

Darla grins at me, showing a heavily coffee stained set of dentures as she sits beside me. "Nice to meet you. I've met your little one. He was with Bailey the last time she took my trash to the curb. Cute little fella. Is he at the community center with the rest of them?"

"Yeah, and it's the first time he's ever been away from home." I take a swallow of my beer. "And the first break I've had in five years," I add with a grin.

"Well, enjoy it. Nobody can be a mom all the time. Still got to be a woman. Drink and get laid, because life goes by fast."

My beer nearly comes out of my nose, but she doesn't

notice. Her attention is focused down the road. "Oh Lord, there goes Gertie in nothing but her pantyhose. Those no good kids of hers are going to have to do something soon. Dementia has taken over. I'll get her home."

"Let me help you." She lays a hand on my arm, her trench coat sleeve brushing against me, as I get to my feet to accompany her.

"Thanks, but it's not a good idea. She always recognizes me for some reason, but if anyone else approaches her she'll freak out."

Denton gives me a nod when I hesitate, so I sit back down. I don't want to make things worse.

"Ow! Get your hand out of my ass!"

"Your ass is the last place I want my hand! Get my arm lost in there and never get it back. Fucking Bermuda Triangle ass."

Everyone turns to watch the show behind us. Trey and Kenny have decided the best way to rig up the lights is to break into the laundry room that's locked at night to plug in the extension cords. Trey is half out of the window, his rather large posterior bulging in the fading light while Kenny tries to stuff him in further.

"I can almost reach it! Another inch!" Trey cries. The sight is funny enough, but once he starts kicking his legs, it reminds me of the cartoons where the characters run in place in mid-air before sprinting away.

Giggles spill out of me, and Neal's face splits into a grin. "Those two are crazy, but they have more fun than anyone I've ever met."

"That's probably true. We might be looking at a Winnie the Pooh situation here, though."

Trey has managed to plug in the cords and is now trying to squeeze back out of the window. He rocks back and forth until the window squirts him out like toothpaste.

Everyone cheers, and he flips us off.

"I thought we were going to have to get some butter," Denton laughs.

"Suck my dick, Dent."

"Sorry dude, I'm allergic to shrimp."

"I'm hung like a horse. Just ask your sister."

"I don't have a sister."

"You will in about nine months." Denton jumps to his feet, and Trey laughs, dodging him and running around.

It always comes back to "I fucked your mother" jokes with those guys, but even I have to admit, that was funny.

Emily waves at me as she approaches. Neal is deep in conversation with a few guys about a Dungeons and Dragons group, so I head over to her.

"Hey, Em, want a beer?" I ask, and she shakes her head.

"Nah, I'm not going to stay long. I have to be at work early." Emily works at the local laundromat. I swear, it seems like half the neighborhood has a job cleaning something. Hotel rooms, cars, laundry. Being poor is a dirty job.

She gestures behind her. "I didn't want to miss this, though."

My gaze follows her hand to find Dennis and Sammy dragging what looks like a large, plastic kiddie pool and a pile of wood behind them. "What are those two idiots doing?" I laugh.

"No idea. But they've been plotting and planning outside my window for a half hour, so I'm sure it'll be epic."

We walk into the playground and take a seat on the swings. "I can't remember the last time I was on a swing," Emily says, grinning and pumping her feet. Of course, because of Aiden, I'm no stranger to them, and it doesn't take me long to catch up to her. The cool night air blows my hair back, drying the sweat on the back of my neck. Between that sensation and the beer, it's like I'm twelve years old again without a care in the world.

"Can I ask you something?" Emily asks.

"I think you just did."

"Ha ha bitch. Something personal."

My feet drag back and forth against the dirt, sending dust billowing through the air, and Emily does the same. "What's up?"

"Does the age difference cause problems with you and Neal? Because there's a guy who comes in my work every week and I can't seem to get him out of my head. But he's at least ten years older, and I'm guessing he has at least three kids."

Struck down by the rumor mill again. "Neal and I aren't together."

A doubting smile crawls over her face. "Okay, so maybe you can't give me relationship advice, but how's the sex? Older guys must be better at it, right?"

Without intending to, I find myself staring at Neal as he laughs and hangs out with the guys. I must be perving on him longer than I think because Emily laughs and adds, "That's a yes."

"No! I mean, I don't know. We aren't sleeping together. We're just friends."

She twists back and forth in the swing like a kid. "Is he gay?"

"No!"

"Are you gay?"

"No!"

"So, he's into you, and you're just clueless. Got it."

I glare at her for a moment, and we both break into laughter. "He's not into me. We're both on our own with a kid. We help each other out. That's all."

"He's looking at you like he'd like to help you out of your clothes."

Neal and Mitch, another neighbor who lives on the opposite end of the circle start toward us. "Hush. Here he comes," I whisper.

"Ladies," Mitch says. I don't know him well. The one-bedroom apartments are on the opposite end of the circle, and it's mostly older or disabled people who live in them. Mitch is around fifty-five if I had to venture a guess, but his eyes roam over me like a greedy teenage boy who just learned how to beat off. "We're going to walk over to the gas station for some cigarettes. Thought you might want to accompany us."

"I'll buy you a candy bar," Neal teases, grinning at me.

I grab my bottle from the ground and take the last few swallows of beer. "I'm not a child. I want a slushy, not candy."

Neal drains his beer, and everyone tosses them in the trash can as we pass. It's not a dry county here anymore, but public drinking is still illegal. No matter how old you are, they can bust you for walking down the road with a beer. Technically, the keg and everything is illegal to be out here like this, but our cops are pretty cool. They know us, and as long as no one is starting trouble, they leave us alone.

The wind picks up, and a shiver runs through me.

Without a word, Neal pulls off his hoodie and hands it to me.

"You don't have to do that. I'm fine."

"And I'm hot. So be warned, it may be a little sweaty."

It's not sweaty, but it smells like him and I hope he doesn't think he's ever getting it back.

The gas station we're heading to is a five-minute walk away. For a split second, I look around for Aiden, then chuckle at myself. It doesn't escape Neal's notice, and he smiles at me. "It feels weird to just go…you know?"

"Do you want me to whine that I can't find my shoes first?"

"Might be helpful. And I'll try to keep you out of traffic."

Laughing, he grabs my hand. I'm twenty-three years old. A man holding my hand should not make me blush like a high schooler. It also shouldn't make my heart speed up, or make me imagine his rough hands in other, far more sensitive places. But it does.

He keeps his hand in mine as we play Frogger through the thin, nighttime traffic to cross the four-lane street. Why isn't he letting go? Why aren't I letting go? Why am I making such a big deal over holding his damned *hand*?

Maybe because it's the most action I've had in five years.

His eyes shine under the bright gas station lights, and the words tumble out of my mouth. "Are you drunk?"

"I've had two beers, V," he scoffs.

"Good. I don't want to take advantage. Of your slushy buying generosity, I mean." Shut up, Veronica. For the love of dick and tater tots, shut up. Not every thought that goes through your head has to spill out your mouth.

"I'm not drunk. I promise I'll remember tonight."

Are those words as loaded as I hear them?

"I'm buying you the slushy. It's completely consensual."

"A consensual slushy." I nod, fighting back a grin. "Sounds perfect."

"What the hell are you two going on about?" Mitch asks. "It feels like I'm watching my sister's kids."

"Don't get your Depends all twisted, Mitch. I'll buy you a slushy too," Neal says.

Emily and I both crack up. I bump my shoulder into his. "Well, now I don't feel special at all. If you're buying for everyone."

"I'll get you a large one."

"She needs a large one," Emily announces as we make our way inside the gas station.

Apparently, Mitch isn't far off. Take away our kids for a night and we all turn into teenagers. It's like we're all just a bunch of children impersonating adults because that's what's expected of us.

We all split up when we get inside as Mitch goes after his cigarettes, and I head to the slushy machine. One beer and I'm already done. Guess maybe I'm an adult after all. After agonizing over raspberry versus cherry, I make a half and half and hunt down Neal.

"I'll never understand how they get away with this shit," he muses, staring at a display in the back.

"Because none of it is technically illegal, and tweakers' stolen money is as green as anyone else's," I reply dryly.

Anyone who has grown up in a bad or poor area knows about this stuff. The glass tubes containing a fake rose and Chore Boy cleaning pads that are used to smoke crack and other drugs. The small cans of spray paint next to cheap, white cotton socks used to huff it. I remember wanting one of those little rose tubes when I was a kid, and Mom saying no. I didn't understand what they were actually used for.

A skinny woman edges past us to pick up a rose pipe, giving us a hectic, snaggle toothed grin as she walks away.

We all meet back up in front of the station and start home.

"That skinny girl was checking you out, Mitch," Emily

teases.

Mitch shudders and shakes his head. “No thanks. She had summer teeth.”

“What?”

“Summer teeth. Some are in her mouth. Some are in her pocket.”

“Don’t be mean!” Emily exclaims, through a mass of giggles.

“Maybe she’s born with it. Maybe it’s methamphetamine,” Neal adds.

Emily and I walk side by side on the way back, chatting about nonsense until Neal says, “What the hell are they doing?”

Yeah, remember the kiddie pool and pallets Dennis and Sammy were dragging out? The pool is now set up to the side of the basketball court. It’s filled with water, and a pallet is supporting a black, metal, burn barrel in the center.

A burn barrel.

Which contains fire.

“Hey! Come on in!” Dennis shouts. “We made a hot tub!”

“That is without a doubt the most redneck shit I’ve ever seen in my life,” I announce, as we join the crowd at the edge of the pool.

“What the hell? Is your family tree a wreath?” Mitch asks.

“I hate to say it, but it seems to work. You know the rule. It isn’t stupid if it works,” Neal points out.

Trey and Kenny both kick off their shoes and step in, laughing at how the barrel sizzles every time the water washes up a little higher on it.

Neal grins down at me. “What? You don’t want to get in?”

“Nope, but knock yourself out.”

A horrible retching sound comes from behind us and we turn to find Samantha puking into the bushes, her man for the night holding back her hair.

I’ve had about enough of Violent Circle for the night and apparently, Neal has too.

“Want to watch a movie?”

“My place,” I agree.

Chapter Six

Neal

Veronica sits back on her couch, sipping her slush. She was so adorable, all freaked out over leaving Aiden. I remember how that felt the first time Bailey slept over at a friend's house, and couldn't resist stepping in. Besides, there's no one else I'd rather spend my childless night with.

"How did Bailey's recital go?" she asks.

"She did fantastic. Never missed a note. Now, that is the last time we're talking about the kids tonight. I'm instituting a rule."

She giggles and folds her legs beneath her. "Deal. I love Aiden to death, but pretending to be young again for a night would be nice."

"You're twenty-three," I point out, perusing her movie collection. "And you have a lot of stoner movies for someone who doesn't smoke."

She shrugs, tucking a strand of hair behind her ear. "I used to smoke, you know, before I got pregnant. It makes me stupid though, so I couldn't do it and take care of Aiden."

"I don't do it often, and only when Bailey isn't around." Grinning, I sit beside her and pull a joint from my pocket. "Kids aren't here tonight, Ms. Senior Citizen."

Her plump lips stretch into a smile. "Says the man pushing

forty."

"Thirty-three is not pushing forty."

She takes the joint and lighter from my hand and sparks it up. "Fine. Pick a movie. But don't say I didn't warn you when I lose a hundred IQ points."

There are times when I'm sure she knows exactly what that smile and laugh does to me, but the next second I'm convinced she's completely naïve when it comes to how I see her. How I want her.

I know the whole neighborhood thinks we have something going on, and it's understandable because we spend so much time together, but I've never done more than give her a hug after a rough day. We help one another out, since each of us is missing a parent to our kids. It really helps for Bailey to have a woman to talk to, and I know she's concerned about Aiden not having a male role model. We all have fun together, but we've left it at that.

A little over two years ago, Bailey lost it when I took my wedding ring off. Her mother had been gone for three years by then, and I knew it was past time, but it still hurt her far worse than I anticipated. That's the reason I don't date. My daughter's happiness comes first, and she needs to grow up a little before I can consider it.

So as hard as it's been, I've restrained myself every time I've wanted to grab Veronica and kiss her until we run out of air. Not to mention, she's so much younger than me. I'm certain she'd rather find a guy her age.

I open the window beside us a few inches to vent the smoke, and we settle on the couch to watch the movie. Silence engulfs the room as the weed takes effect.

Her fiery hair hangs in waves around her heart shaped face, and her big blue eyes never leave the screen. She really does zone out. Out of nowhere, she bursts out laughing at something that happens in the movie. Maybe if I was watching it instead of staring at the light sprinkling of freckles trailing down her neck and disappearing under her collar, I'd know what it was. Damn, how long have I been staring at her? It feels like about fifteen minutes, but I know that can't be true. This stuff is potent.

When she stops laughing, she leans her head against my shoulder. “We’re not doing this right.”

My struggling brain tries to read way too much into that statement before she adds, “We should’ve got some chips or ice cream or something.”

“We could order a pizza.”

She sits up with a grin. “Or I could make waffles! Don’t waffles sound amazing?”

They do actually, but we’re stoned. You could give me a piece of bread and it would be the most delicious thing I’ve ever eaten.

I hit pause on the movie, get to my feet, and offer her my hand. “Let’s make waffles.”

Her hand slides into mine, and she stands up. “I have batter already made in the fridge. So it’ll be easy.”

You would think so.

Cooking while high is never recommended.

She plugs in the waffle iron, heats it, adds the batter, then sets a timer. “They take about four minutes each.”

We talk and laugh while she makes the waffles, setting a timer each time until she’s down to the last one. I’m busy getting us something to drink when she says, “Shit. I forgot to set the timer. No idea how long the last one has been cooking. I’ll just say three minutes and hope it doesn’t burn.”

“You wait until the last one to screw up?” I tease, and she throws a dish towel at me.

“I didn’t screw up. It’ll be fine. I’m not even high anymore.”

Those words become a lot funnier when the timer goes off, and she opens the waffle iron.

It’s empty.

I can’t help it. Laughter bursts from my chest.

“Well, you didn’t burn anything. Maybe because the batter is still in the bowl.”

I don’t know exactly what it is that erodes the last of my self-control. Maybe it’s the way her cheeks flush pink and she curls her lips inward, fighting a smile, or the words “Well, fuck,” coming from those lips. Dick sucking lips, we called them when I was young. Maybe the weed lowered my resistance, but either way, I can't fight it.

A soft gasp leaves her as I step into her space, and she steps back, her shoulders pressed against the wall. A hand lands on my chest, and her mouth opens to say something, but she doesn't get the chance before I slip my hand behind her neck and finally get a taste of her lips.

Her body melts into mine. There's no hesitation on her part, like she's been thinking about this as much as I have. I hope that's true because I don't plan on stopping at a kiss.

Her hand wanders over my chest as her other glides down my back to grab my ass. Hard. Fuck, this girl is going to kill me. She comes off as innocent with those youthful looks and wide eyes, but I can feel the passion burning inside her now.

A soft whimper when I slip my tongue between her lips makes my cock twitch, and I can't wait to hear the sounds she makes when she comes. She presses her hips forward, rubbing against my leg, and I can feel the heat of her through the leggings she wears.

"Off," she mumbles, grabbing the bottom of my shirt, and she doesn't have to ask twice. Her lips move across my chest, and I pull her shirt over her head. I knew she wasn't wearing a bra. I've never seen such beautiful tits, pearl white like the rest of her skin, with a dusting of tiny freckles. A small red birthmark rests on the side of her left nipple, and she takes a deep breath when I run my tongue over it before planting my mouth over her nipple.

Her hands tug at my hair. "Neal," she breathes.

"Tell me to stop, V."

"I can't."

More glorious words were never spoken, and I'm right there with her because I can't stop either. "I might come just from you touching me," she adds, as if it's a warning.

"Yeah? Let's see about that."

I slip my hands down the front of her leggings and panties, and she isn't kidding. She's wet and ready, her hips bucking forward at the lightest touch. It's the sexiest fucking thing I've ever seen, and I have no intention of making her come with my hand.

Kissing her neck, I slip my hands under the waistband of her panties and pull them off as I kneel in front of her. She groans at the soft kisses I place on her lower belly, and I steal a glance at her face before I move down. Her slightly parted lips are puffy and red, and her breasts rise and fall quickly with her fast breaths. She doesn't say anything, but her eyes plead with me not to stop.

No worries there.

I grab her ankle and scoot her feet apart as she watches, rapt.

"Yes," she moans, when my tongue finds its target.

Her nails run gently over my scalp, and I grip her hips, holding her in place as I lick and suck at her. In less than a minute, I feel her getting close, and I slide a finger inside her. It catches her off guard, and she cries out, her body shaking inside and out. I need to feel that on my cock. Now.

Her eyes are glassy, and I know it isn't the weed. Fuck drunk looks good on her, and I can't wait to get her to the bedroom.

I stand and open my mouth to speak, but the strangest thing seems to come out. "Mom. Mom. Mom. Mommy. Mommy. Mama. Mama."

Okay, I absolutely did not say that because how fucking creepy would that be? Besides, the voice is clearly Stewie from the Family Guy TV show.

Her eyes meet mine and she dissolves into laughter, which was not at all how I saw this going. "It's my phone. My ringtone. Aiden chose it."

I step back, and she heads to the living room to grab her phone. "Hello? Hey, buddy. Are you having fun?"

Cock blocked by the kid.

I grab two bottles of water from her fridge and follow her, my hard-on leading the way.

She's sitting on the couch, naked, talking on the phone.

"Okay, good night. Be good. I love you too."

She ends the call and looks up at me. "Sorry, he wouldn't go to sleep without saying good night."

She reaches for a throw blanket, and I grab her hand before she can cover herself. “Do you want to call it a night?” I ask.

Her tongue darts out to wet her lips, and her gaze sweeps over my chest, down to the obvious bulge in my pants. “We should.” Her actions don’t match her words because her hand has found its way between my legs.

“I disagree.”

Swallowing hard, she says, “It doesn’t have to mean anything. One time, while our kids are gone.”

“One night,” I correct, knowing damn well I’m lying through my teeth. “As many times as we want.”

“Then we stay friends.”

“Absolutely.” I’m not young or naïve enough to think this won’t change things. That ship sailed the second I kissed her. I have no idea what will happen tomorrow or the next day, but tonight, I’m going to watch her come beneath me.

“I have a birth control implant and I haven’t been with anyone in a long time.”

“Same here, minus the birth control implant.”

She chuckles and shakes her head, then squeals when I scoop her up. “We have about fifteen hours until we have to get the kids. Let’s see how many orgasms we can fit in.”

I place her on the bed, and she watches me remove my jeans and underwear.

“Fuck.” The curse is soft, barely audible, but the way she’s looking at my cock isn’t subtle. She’s nervous. All men want to think they’ve got a giant anaconda even if they’re actually carrying around a pinworm, but I’ve always been happy with my size. Above average, but not a cervix crusher.

Her gaze flits up to mine as I crawl over her. “It really has been a long time for me,” she whispers.

“How long?”

“Over five years.”

I freeze, blinking a few times. I did not expect that. Her cheeks turn pink, and she shrugs. “Not since before I had Aiden. I haven’t had the time or opportunity to get close to anyone since.”

She tilts her head as I brush her hair back. “Are you sure

you want to do this?"

"Pshh, didn't you hear me? Over five years, Neal. If you don't fuck me, I'm going over to Samantha's. She never has a shortage of men."

With a growl, I kiss the teasing smile from her face. "Not...fucking...happening," I say, punctuating each word with a kiss.

She wraps her legs around my ass, and I slide inside her. She's tight, and I can feel her tensing up for a few seconds before she relaxes. "Go slow," she breathes.

Good damn thing because it hasn't been as long for me as for her, but it's still been long enough for me to embarrass myself, especially if she keeps making those soft whimpers.

Kissing her, I pull out and push in slow and careful, feeling her pulse around me as her body adjusts. "We've got all night," I murmur.

Too bad I already know that won't be enough.

Chapter Seven

Veronica

For the first time in years, I wake up slowly instead of being jarred awake by an alarm or Aiden. I climb through the levels of consciousness in increments until I'm aware of the soft bed beneath me and the warm body against my back. Neal's arm is draped over me, and when I open my eyes, his hand lies near my face. Maybe I'm just tired, or still a little spaced out from the weed last night, but I spend a long minute just staring at it.

I've always had a thing for a man's hands. And Neal's are a great example of why. Large and strong, with long fingers. Absently, I slide my hand under his to feel his smooth palm and slightly rougher fingers. Those hands were all over me last night, touching me inside and out, until I was left in a blissed out fog of post orgasmic exhaustion.

I had no idea sex could be that amazing. I was seventeen when I got pregnant and I had only been with Clint, whose idea of great sex was kissing for two minutes then bending me over something.

Neal took his time, touched, kissed, licked, and drove me insane with more orgasms than I thought I was capable of. And I spent just as much time exploring his body, reveling in the moans and hisses he made, especially when my lips were around his cock.

His cock.

It deserves an award. I could write poetry about it. Ode to the perfect penis. Or maybe a Haiku. Isn't it five syllables, seven syllables, five syllables?

Smooth and glorious
Grace my vagina again
With your stiff magic

Nah, that one sounds creepy.

Leaning to the left
Extravagantly swollen
I shall call you Rod

Yeah, that's better.

I'm lost in my ridiculous thoughts when Neal's arm tightens around me. It's possible he's awake because I was wiggling my ass against him, but in my defense, he started it with that morning hard-on prodding me.

"Good morning," he murmurs, running his thumb back and forth across my navel.

"Morning."

It's painfully silent for a few moments while a war rages in my head. Last night wasn't enough. I want him again, and we have time. But I'm also clear headed today and I know this has been a mistake we'll probably regret later.

He rests his chin on my shoulder. "I can hear those wheels spinning in your head, V. Say what you need to."

"Everything goes back to normal today."

"Yes."

"After a morning quickie." There goes my ass again, pressing against him, being all greedy. I've lost control of it.

Chuckling, he plants a kiss on the back of my neck, and grabs my knee, pushing my leg forward. His hand trails down over my ass before he slips a thick finger inside me. I'm already wet and ready, so he doesn't hesitate to add another finger. We stay right like that, on our sides with his body pressed to mine while he moves them slowly, in and out, his fingertips dragging over that sweet spot just right to make me moan and squirm. Damn, he's good at this. Clint used to finger me like there was a lottery ticket in there he had to scratch off.

He withdraws his hand and shifts his hips until his cock is between my legs. In one firm thrust, he buries himself inside me, and I can't help the cry that leaves my throat. It's deep this way. Hot, licking kisses rain down on my neck and shoulders as he fucks me in a slow, steady, mind blowing rhythm.

I turn my head and find his lips, kissing him as my hand reaches back, running over every bit of him I can reach. "Neal." His name falls from my lips, and his eyes burn into mine. The combination of the way he's making me feel and the intensity of his gaze on mine is too much, too intimate, and I have to close my eyes.

"Does that feel good?" he murmurs.

"God, yes. Harder," I plead.

Rising up over me a little, he grabs my hand that's reaching for him and pins it, along with the other, to the bed. I'm trapped , rolled so far on my side I'm nearly on my stomach. Hard, fast thrusts send streaks of pleasure through me, faster and faster until they're piling up, building to a height I've never felt and not sure I can handle. Just as I'm ready to plead for mercy, I'm rocked by a surge of spasms that reduces me to an incoherent mess. All I can do is grip his hand that still holds mine down as I ride out the wonderfully devastating attack on all my senses.

This man just owned me. Took my body and made it do things I didn't know it was capable of.

Fuck.

Our heavy breathing is the only sound in the room as we both recover. He slips out of me, then pulls me back against his chest, holding me like I may make a run for it. It's tempting, because I'm torn between asking him to fuck me like that every day until I'm old and crotchety, and hating him because this is supposed to be a one-day casual thing, but he made me feel way too much. Stupid emotions will screw everything up. I don't want to be that girl who can't get laid without turning all psycho. And I could. The way I feel now, I want to climb his cock, plant a flag on top, and claim Mount Pecker in the name of Veronica, marking it for my own use only.

"Are you okay?" he asks, kissing my neck.

Space. I need space.

"Yeah, I'm good." He releases me as I wiggle away, and I can feel his eyes on my back as I rummage through my dresser for clean clothes. "I'm going to take a quick shower before I have to pick up Aiden." Without looking at him or giving him a chance to respond, I flee to the bathroom, locking the door behind me.

One night. It was one hell of an amazing night, but it's over, and I need to get a grip. Neal has been a wonderful friend to me, and Aiden is crazy about him and Bailey, so I can't screw this up by acting weird just because we licked each other's genitals.

It's decided then. I won't be weird. I guess that starts now since I just ran away and locked the bathroom door behind me, but I can't have him in the shower with me. We did that last night and the sight of his sexy, lean body is already imprinted deeply in my brain.

As the water washes the smell of our night from my skin, I close my eyes, and try to get a grip. I'm twenty-three years old. I should be perfectly capable of having some casual sex without freaking out like a smitten teenage girl over an older guy.

I can do this.

Just maintain, girl.

My little self pep talk seems to help until I leave the bathroom and find Neal sitting on the edge of the bed, pulling on his shoes. He looks up at me with concern. "V, are we okay?"

"Of course." I force a smile. "We had a little naked fun while the kids were gone. It's no big deal. Everything is fine."

Skepticism is written all over his face, but he nods anyway, and drops a kiss on my forehead as he leaves the room. "Bailey just called. Do you want me to pick up Aiden while I'm there and save you the trip?"

"No thanks. I have some stuff to do, so I'll pick him up in a few."

He stops at the front door, then strides back over and pulls me into a hug. My response is automatic. My arms tighten around him and my face burrows into his neck while I breathe in his scent that is suddenly so alluring.

My racing heart calms, and I can feel my muscles relax. He steps back and grins down at me. "I have to work tomorrow. How about we grill out after I get home?"

"Sounds good. I'll make some baked macaroni. Bailey loves it." See, everything is right back to normal. No harm done.

I release the breath I was holding as soon as the door falls shut behind him.

Neal's car is still at the community center a few minutes later when I show up to get Aiden. My head really isn't in the right place to talk to him again right now, but I have to act like everything is normal.

Noble, Jani, Wyatt, and Neal all stand together, talking with a woman I don't recognize. Aiden and Eddie are racing around them, laughing. It looks like they're getting along better, at least. Jani waves at me as I enter, and Neal gives me a smile that makes my stomach dip and rise.

As I approach, the other woman turns to me and crosses her arms. She looks at me like I'm tracking in dog shit or something. I don't know what her problem is, but I am not in the mood.

"You're Aiden's mother?" she demands.

So, I guess we're just skipping the niceties. "I'm Veronica, and yes, Aiden is my son."

I barely get the words out before she points a finger in my face. Jani's eyebrows jump up, and she calls to the kids to join her to get their stuff together, leading them away. She knows me well enough to know this won't be pretty.

See, I'm the most laid-back person you'd ever want to meet,

but that doesn't mean I take shit, especially when it comes to my kid. I'm not one of those parents that thinks my kid can do no wrong, and I make him apologize if he misbehaves in public or wrongs someone, but I don't care if Aiden pissed on this woman's feet, she has no right getting in my face.

"Well, you need to speak to your son! He told my Manny that—"

"First." I interrupt, taking a step toward her, which makes her retreat a step. "Get your finger out of my face. Second, don't tell me I need to do anything. If there's been some disagreement between our kids, we can discuss it like adults, which usually begins with an introduction."

Her lips purse, but I can see a bit of fear along with annoyance. "I'm Madison Blue."

"What did Aiden do, Mrs. Blue?"

Neal, Wyatt, and Noble are all watching, and judging by the way they're trying not to smile, this isn't going to be good.

Mrs. Blue glances around at her audience and huffs, "Manny was trying to talk about Jesus and the story of Easter when Aiden began using foul language."

Shit.

There's some foul language for her. We aren't religious, so whatever Aiden said to offend her was probably innocent, but I'm surprised he was swearing. He never does that.

"What did he say?"

Noble snorts, covers his mouth, and looks away as Mrs. Blue struggles to answer. Her mouth opens and closes multiple times.

"Feel free to spell it," I invite. It's so ridiculous. She's like forty years old and she can't swear?

Stepping closer, she hisses, "He said penis!"

It takes me a moment to process, since I was expecting an actual swear word, not a body part. "I-what did he say?"

"I'm not saying it again!" She glares at me.

"No, I heard you. He said penis. It's the context I'm not clear on."

"He was talking nasty. He told Manny that Jesus had a

penis."

Neal loses it, his body shaking as he tries to conceal it. It doesn't help that Wyatt can't stop smiling. He owns this place so I'm glad he's not all pissed off over this.

Catching Aiden's eye, I wave him over, and Mrs. Blue calls for her kid. I swear, there are some conversations you never think you'll have to have. And not discussing religious figures' genitals has to be near the top of the list.

"Aiden, Mrs. Blue said you were talking about penises," I tell him.

His eyes widen, and he gazes around at everyone listening. I can remember that feeling from when I was a kid, how awful it was to get in trouble in front of people. Kneeling down to his level, I continue. "You aren't in trouble. I'm just trying to figure out what's going on. What were you talking about?"

Aiden inches toward Neal, and his hand unconsciously attaches to the outer leg of Neal's jeans. "You said that all boys have penises."

We did have this conversation lately. He's five. These are normal questions for him to have. I just should've made it clear it's not an appropriate topic elsewhere.

"Manny told me that Jesus was a guy who came back from the dead for Easter. If Jesus is a boy, then he has a penis."

This is what she's all worked up over? I mean, technically, he's right. Mrs. Blue gives me an expectant look, like she's hoping I'll tear into my kid.

"Listen, Ade, you're right. Boys have penises. But there are some things that aren't always appropriate to talk about."

"Like vaginas too?"

There's not a person within earshot that's not laughing now, but I manage to keep a straight face.

"What's a vagina?" Manny asks, speaking up for the first time.

"Don't say that!" Mrs. Blue snaps, and he takes a step back.

"I'm sorry! I didn't know it was a bad word." Poor kid.

"It's not, a vagina is what girls have instead of a penis," Aiden explains, as if he's a pro on the subject.

"Nuh-uh!" Manny cries. "Girls don't have nothing! Their butts just go all the way around!"

"Manny! Go wait in the lobby. Now!"

Swallowing back a chuckle, I grab Aiden's hand and look him in the eye. "It's not appropriate to talk about this stuff in public. If you have questions about private parts, you come and talk to me, okay?"

"Okay."

"Why don't you go hang with Bailey for a minute until I'm ready to go?"

Smiling, he nods and bounces off in her direction.

Mrs. Blue glares at me as she realizes I'm not punishing my kid for an innocent—and frankly, funny—mistake. "Maybe if you attended church occasionally, your kid would know how to act in polite society."

This bitch did not.

I give her my best smile when I reply. "Maybe if you got some penis every now and then you could pull that giant stick out of your ass and not be such a prude. If you can't get a real one, Scarlet Toys has a wide selection."

Her jaw drops, and she glances around at everyone, clearly expecting someone to come to her defense. When all she gets are shrugs and snorts of laughter, she stalks away without another word.

"I'm sorry. I will talk to Aiden," I tell Wyatt, who is wiping tears from his eyes.

"It's fine. He's a kid. It wasn't a big deal."

I join in the laughter as everyone loses it again.

This is my life as a mom.

Jesus penis.

For fuck's sake.

"Stop in the office before you leave," Wyatt tells me. "Cassidy wants to talk to you about something."

Great. My kid has probably been telling people his penis sticks up sometimes, since that was another uncomfortable conversation that took place recently.

Leaving Aiden to hang out with Bailey for another minute,

I find Cassidy waiting in the office. "Come in," she calls with a smile. "How have you been?"

"Good, how about you?"

"Can't complain. I wanted to see if you might be interested in sending Aiden to our Pre-K program. We're going to start offering it year-round, so it would work like a daycare through the summer, but they'll still be learning."

Sending Aiden to preschool instead of dragging him to work with me would make both of our lives better, but I know I can't afford it. Even the cheapest daycare services charge almost half my salary, and I don't have much to spare.

"That sounds great, and I appreciate you thinking of us, but I can't afford it at the moment."

Cassidy flashes a smile. "The program is new and we're still finding our feet, but we want it to be a positive force in Morganville. Five spots are reserved for low income families. I'd like to offer Aiden one of those spots. There's no cost. We'll be open from seven a.m. to seven p.m. Monday through Saturday. So, he'd be welcome anytime between those hours."

Her words permeate my tired brain, and I sink into the chair in front of her desk. "You're offering me free daycare?"

"Yes. I spent some time with Aiden last night, and he really enjoyed being here. I think he'd fit in perfectly."

My mind is spinning, and I have to push the burst of pride out of the way. The same pride that won't allow me to accept welfare payments or food stamps. It killed me to move to Violent Circle because I knew the place was known for being the poor side of town, but there wasn't any choice involved there. It was the only way to keep a roof over our heads.

Cassidy leans across the desk and lays a hand on mine. "I know what you're feeling. I used to live in the same apartment you do, remember? We all helped each other, and I know from Jani that you do the same for neighbors who need you. This isn't charity or a handout. You work hard, and your kid deserves an education and a chance to be with kids his age. Money shouldn't get in the way of that."

Swallowing hard, I nod. "Thank you so much. If you need

parent volunteers—"

Her head falls back as she laughs and leans back. "Oh, we absolutely do. Once he gets settled in, I'll get with you and we'll see in what ways you can help."

"Okay. What do I need to sign him up?"

"We just need to see his shot records to make sure he's up to date on vaccinations." She whips out a piece of paper and hands it to me. "Here is the overview of the program, how we'll handle lunch and snacks, field trips, etc. He can start on Monday if you like."

"He'll be here."

"Eddie is starting Monday as well, and they're moving onto Violent Circle this week, so he'll have a friend here his first day," Cassidy remarks, scribbling on a paper.

Or a frenemy, I think, biting back a smile. Wait until Aiden finds out Eddie is going to be his neighbor as well. "Thanks again. I'll bring the paperwork in with him on Monday."

We manage to make it out of the community center without any further drama. Aiden climbs in the backseat, then groans when he sees the baskets full of laundry.

"Sorry, kiddo. It needs done. I brought your tablet and snacks."

Usually, I hate the laundromat as much as he does, but Emily is working today, and I need to talk to someone.

At least the place isn't busy. After I get Aiden settled in at a table with a bag of chips, juice box, and his tablet, I load up the washers with this week's dirty clothes. What I'd give for a washer and dryer at home.

Aiden is lost in the world of his cartoons when Emily waves me over. She's working behind the counter, ironing a stack of shirts.

"Hungover?" she teases.

"Nah, I only drank one beer."

Her lips twitch as she runs the iron across a collar. "I saw Neal leaving your place this morning." Yeah, I'm sure half the neighborhood did. She continues. "Is this where you swear he slept on the couch and you're just friends?"

"No," I sigh, glancing back to make sure no one is in earshot. "This is where I tell you he fucked my brains out, and all I can think about is having him again."

"It's about damned time."

"It was a mistake. It won't happen again."

"Is that you talking or him?" Emily sets down her work, grabs a soda from the table and comes around the counter to stand beside me.

"Both of us. We agreed it was a one-night thing."

"So, you're both idiots."

I shove her. "No, we both have kids we have to consider."

Emily stares at Aiden. "Look, I can't speak as a parent, but I've seen Aiden with Neal. He adores him. And I know Bailey is close to you."

"And we can keep it that way. But if we tried to date and it didn't work out, we could ruin that."

Emily nods. "I see where you're coming from, but, I think it's too late for those kinds of worries now. You've already been together, you won't be satisfied with a friendship anymore. I've been there."

That's what I'm worried about.

"I'm just going to act like nothing ever happened, and I'm sure he'll do the same."

"Let me know how that works out." She grabs my arm and whispers. "That's the guy I was telling you about. No ring, but always washes a bunch of kid's clothes. Isn't he sexy?"

He is. And his gaze searches out Emily. Smiling, he nods at her, and I swear she practically dissolves into a puddle beside me. "What do you know about him? Other than he wants in your panties?"

She swats at me. "He does not. I don't know anything about him. I've never spoken to him, other than a passing hello."

"So, go talk to him."

She scoffs. "Yeah, because it's that easy. I'll just walk up and offer him some fabric softener. Besides, he's probably got a brood of kids and he must have ten years on me."

It's probably closer to fifteen, but the guy is as fit as any twenty-five-year-old. The only real sign of his age is the gray that peppers his hair and beard.

"Have we decided we're both just going to be spinsters and live with a load of cats, then?" I ask.

"It's looking more likely. Uh...Veronica?" Emily tilts her head in the mystery man's direction, and I see Aiden heading this way.

"Shit. I have to go before he starts talking about Jesus penis."

Emily blinks and exclaims. "What?"

"It's a long story."

Chapter Eight

Neal

It's only been a week and it's clear the whole no sex with Veronica plan isn't going to work. No matter how much I tell myself that she's a young mother who doesn't need me complicating things, I can't stop thinking about her. Her smile, her laugh, the way she scratches her jaw with her pointer finger when she's nervous or thinking.

Sex with her was way better than I ever imagined, and my imagination is pretty vivid. I want her again. Maybe I could resist if I knew she didn't want the same thing, but she does. It's obvious in the way she watches me when she thinks I don't see. She goes out of her way not to touch me, even in innocent ways, when she never cared before. She's trying to pull away to keep control which just makes me want her more.

Things are complicated since neither of us think dating would be good for our kids, so I have a new plan that I'm determined to get her on board with. We've both been sex deprived for too long. We need to get it out of our systems. So, we'll just take our opportunities when the kids are gone or asleep. It's not the kind of relationship I pictured having at my age, but I also didn't foresee raising a girl alone and having to put her emotional well-being above my own. If it weren't for Bailey, I would be all in with Veronica, but I have to put my little girl first.

The last few years have been lonely. I've filled the time working extra hours, and hanging out with the guys from my poker group here and there, but the older Bailey gets the less she needs me. It leaves a lot of time to miss the things I've tried to block out since her mother left. I've rediscovered a lot of those small joys with Veronica. Little things like eating dinner together, laughing over the kids' antics, having good natured arguments over T.V. shows. I want her in my bed, but I want her in my daily life more. I have to find a way to make this work.

It's a beautiful Sunday and I have the day off, so I fire up the grill and text Veronica.

Me: Hamburgers, ribs, and chicken at my house.
Her: On my way home. Be over after I shower.
Me: Stop making me picture you naked.

After a minute or two, I know she isn't going to respond to that. Maybe because she's driving, but more likely she doesn't know what to say. We haven't talked about that night since it happened, but I'm not willing to keep pretending it didn't.

Aiden rushes around the side of my apartment a few minutes later. "Hey Neal! Mom said to tell you she'll be here in a few minutes. Me and Eddie are going to the park!"

He rushes off again before I can reply. I peek around the corner and watch as Eddie joins him, and they enter the playground. There are plenty of other kids there, including Bailey and her friend Amber, who spent the night last night, so they're fine.

I hope they stay over there for a bit while I have a little discussion with Veronica.

She pops around the corner a few minutes later, a covered bowl in her hands. "I made some potato salad last night."

"Sounds good."

Damn, look at her. Wet hair pulled into a ponytail, jean shorts that end right under her ass, and a clingy shirt that shows off her small curves. "I'll just put it in the fridge," she says, and steps through the back door.

I follow her inside. She turns, shutting the fridge door, and stops when she sees me standing there. "Damn it, Neal! You scared the hell out of me!"

Her lips are open in surprise, and I can't stand it anymore. My hand threads into her hair, and I plant my mouth on hers before she can react. It's the moment when I know for sure I'm not in this alone, because she doesn't hesitate for even a second before kissing me back and it's filled with the same amount of passion and desperation I feel.

Her arms wrap around me, and my other hand cups her ass in those little shorts.

"The kids," she gasps when we finally break apart, and I kiss down her neck.

"Are at the park."

Her tongue dives back into my mouth, and I slide my hand under her shirt, feeling the warm, smooth skin of her stomach.

"We can't." Her actions don't match her words. She presses her hips forward into mine as I run a thumb over her nipple, through her thin bra.

"The kids don't have to know. We'll just take advantage of times like this." Closing her eyes, she groans as I suck the sensitive spot below her ear. "It's driving me crazy not to touch you, V. Tell me you feel the same way."

"You're all I think about when I—" She stops herself. Caught up in the moment, she almost said something she didn't mean to reveal.

"When you what? Tell me."

Her cheeks flame. "When I use my vibrator."

Fucking hell, is she trying to kill me? My cock is rock hard in my pants, and I'm standing in the kitchen where the kids could pop in at any minute. Stepping back a bit, I press my forehead to hers. "Jesus, V. That's the sexiest fucking thing I've ever heard."

We stay that way for a few moments before she asks, "You want to sneak around like teenagers hiding from their parents?"

"Is that too weird and immature?"

"No, just clarifying," she says, kissing me again.

The thwack of the front screen door slamming shut makes

us both take a step back, and I grab a stack of paper plates to hold in front of my crotch. Veronica quickly turns and pretends to be rustling in the fridge as Bailey steps in. "Amber's dad just picked her up."

"Okay, well, dinner will be ready in about an hour."

Bailey's gaze bounces between us as Veronica shuts the fridge and smiles at her. "I'm going back to the park." Her tone makes it clear she thinks something is up, but a second later, she's out the door.

"This is crazy," Veronica says through a grin.

"Absolutely insane," I agree.

The back door opens and this time it's Aiden. "Are we eating soon? I'm starving."

Forgetting why I'm holding the stack of paper plates, I hand them to him. "Pretty soon. Why don't you take these outside?"

My hard-on has lessened a bit, but the shorts I'm wearing do little to conceal it.

Aiden grins up at me. "That happens to me sometimes too. Peeing helps," he announces before scampering out the back door.

Veronica bursts out laughing, and I rub my forehead. "I just got erection advice from a preschooler."

"Well, he was worried there was something wrong with him, so you set his mind at ease, if that makes you feel better."

"Not even a little. Come on." I grab her arm and lead us to the back door. "We will never speak of this again."

"I can't promise the same for Aiden."

Fantastic.

It's been an interesting day. My meeting with the pro bono lawyer has a smile plastered across my face. He's pissed. And a pissed off lawyer is a good thing to have on your side. He's filing a lawsuit on behalf of the tenants for multiple things, but the main case is about management taking tenant's belongings and selling them back to them. Apparently, owning a property doesn't give you the right to steal from your renters.

It will take some time to make its way to court, assuming they fight it instead of changing their policies, but at least we have someone on our side. I wanted to do this before I end up moving, and it looks like a great time since I just received my updated credit report. After years of trying to pay off all the debt my ex-wife left me in, I've finally succeeded.

My credit has crept up from good to excellent, and I have a nice nest egg in savings. It's taken me longer than I expected, but I got here all the same. My next appointment was with the loan officer at the bank. He's no stranger to me since we went to school together and he's had my information on hold until I could qualify for the amount required to purchase the house and business. When he told me I was good to go, that I could make an offer, I almost kissed him.

Now it's time for a talk with George, the owner of Jetsky's Car Wash. George hired me over ten years ago. I spent years working my way up from doing windows and interiors, to drying and vacuuming, to management. He has always said that he'd be happy for me to take over the place when he's ready to retire, and last year he started hinting that his retirement wouldn't be far away.

It's one of the reasons it took me so long to pay off all the debt I was left with. I could've put more toward it, and less in savings to pay it off quicker, but I knew this day was going to come. I've seen what Jetsky's nets per month, and it's far more than I'll ever make as a manager.

The biggest draw about this plan is that when George sells, it won't just be the business. He built the car wash right across the street from his home. He plans to sell both and move to be closer to his kids and grandkids, so I'm hoping to make an offer on both. If Jetsky's continues to do well, I'll have no problem paying on both mortgages. If it doesn't, I'll be filing bankruptcy and back on Violent Circle, but I have to try.

"Neal, good to see you," George exclaims, as I take a seat

beside him at the bar. He spends a few evenings a week at this little tavern, so I wasn't surprised when he had me meet him here.

"You too. What trouble have you been causing?"

Laughing, he tips a wink at the thin, pale skinned bartender. "Just trying to convince this beautiful lady here I still have some fuel left in the tank."

"I don't doubt you have gas, you dirty old man. Go blow it somewhere else," she says, wiping down the bar.

Turning to me, he takes a drink of beer. "That woman loves me. Hates it when I'm not here."

"You're never not here, George," she says, setting another beer in front of him.

"I'll have the same, thanks," I tell her. I've been here a couple of times so this isn't the first time I've seen the good natured exchange between them. George is a likable guy who gets along with everyone. Every now and then, he'll cross that line into raunchy territory, but if anyone gets offended, the *I'm just a feeble old man who doesn't understand what he's saying* act seems to work for him. It's hilarious because the guy is sharp as hell.

"You said you wanted to talk. If you're here to tell me you're quitting, just turn your ass right around now."

Ice cold beer hits the spot today, and I'm ready to celebrate a little. "Actually, I came to send you off to pasture. You're looking a little ragged, George. You need some of your daughter's home cooking to set you straight."

He cocks his head to look at me, suddenly a lot more interested in what I have to say. "It's about damned time. Not the home cooking. My girl can't boil rice without setting the house on fire. But I was wondering if you'd ever shit or get off the pot." George laughs his wheezy laugh.

"Are you still asking the same amount?"

"Yup. Papers are all drawn up. Been collecting dust in my desk drawer for the last few years."

"Are you okay with me sending a home inspector over to make sure there's nothing major wrong?"

"Knock yourself out. I wouldn't want the roof to fall on your ugly head once you're in there."

"Then you've got a deal."

It will take a couple of months to get everything ironed out with the handover of the business and house, but George calls me a few days after our meeting to tell me the inspector found no problems and I'd be getting paperwork to that effect in the mail.

"I'm taking a trip in a couple of weeks down to see my daughter and find a nice apartment."

"Be careful, old timer."

"Fuck off. I'm in my prime."

"Tell that to the cop when he sees your driver's license is written in hieroglyphics."

His cackle rings through the air so loud, I have to hold the phone back. "You know you've got a month's worth of vacation time coming to you. You should take some time off and use it. Once you're the boss, you may not get the chance again."

It's not a bad idea. I'd love a little free time, especially because I know once I take over, I'm going to be working my ass off to make this a success and to pay off the loans. "Are you sure you can do without me?"

"I'll get Jim to cover your shifts. So, go away. I don't want to see you for two weeks."

"I guess I could take Bailey to visit my parents."

"Or go to Vegas and get laid. They have escorts who won't care about your unfortunate face."

"Fuck off, old man. Call me if you need me. Try not to kill the business before I get back."

We trade a few more insults before hanging up. I really am going to miss that guy.

I'm thrilled to see Veronica's car is home when I turn onto Violent Circle. I didn't want to tell her about the business or house until everything was final in case it all fell apart for some reason. Now, I can't wait to tell her everything.

"V?" I call out, tapping on her door.

"Come in!"

I step into the living room and she emerges from the hall in a pair of shorts and a thin, clingy t-shirt, her hair wrapped up in a towel on her head. "Sorry. I just got out of the shower."

"Don't be sorry," I murmur, running my hands up her sides, over the soft material. She hums when I lean down to kiss her neck.

"Don't start anything we can't finish, you tease. Bailey's bus is going to let off any minute."

"I'm aware. But you can't come out here looking like that and expect me to keep my hands off of you." I settle for giving her a quick kiss, then take a step back before I end up dragging her into the bedroom, kids be damned. "I have some big news."

"Yeah? Good, I hope." She takes a seat and whips the towel off her head, using it to dry her long locks.

"Really good. My bank approved me for the loans I told you about."

Her mouth falls open. "You're buying Jetsky's?"

Sitting beside her, I nod, a wide smile on my face. "In a month or so, I'll be the owner."

Her squeal fills the room, and she throws her arms around me. "I'm so happy for you! I know how long you've worked and saved for this."

I can't remember the last time I felt this happy. My life is finally heading in the right direction, and I have someone who is genuinely happy for me. Of course, my parents will be thrilled too, but this is different. I know my feelings for V have surpassed any kind of friendship, but our little arrangement makes it difficult to know if she feels the same. I'm terrified I might be falling in love with her, but at this moment, with her arms wrapped around me, and her words of approval and happiness in my ear, I don't care.

Life is long, wonderful, and horrific. If you can find someone who makes the bad parts bearable and the good parts better, you should hold onto that person with everything you have because it's a rare gift not everyone is given.

"I'm also buying his house. I don't know exactly when yet, but we'll be moving."

Her smile is a little reluctant, and I understand. If it were the other way around, I'd be disappointed too. "That's so amazing. Does Bailey know yet? She's going to be thrilled."

"Not yet. I'm going to talk to her when she gets home. George also gave me the next two weeks off, so I can sneak in a little rest before everything gets crazy. I'm going to take her to visit my parents in Illinois. We'll probably stay a couple of days."

"There's the bus now," she points out, and I get to my feet. "This doesn't change anything, V. We'll still see each other all the time."

A quick shadow seems to cloud her face before it's replaced by a smile. "Damn right. I know where you're moving to. Now go tell your girl and make her day."

"Grandma!" Bailey shrieks, nearly knocking my mother over with her hug.

"Lordy, girl, you're taller than me!" Mom hugs her and kisses the top of her head before coming over to hug me.

"You have to bring this girl to visit more often. She's growing up too fast!"

"I tried to stop feeding her, but she still kept growing."

"Oh, hush." She slaps me on the shoulder. "Come on in and sit down. We were just talking about your wonderful news."

"The new house has a screened porch where I can play my guitar," Bailey tells her excitedly, after hugging her grandpa as well.

"I'm in the middle of making a roast for dinner. Why don't you come help and tell me all about it," Mom offers, and Bailey follows her back to the kitchen.

Dad sits in his usual spot in the recliner. He reaches down to the mini fridge he has wedged between the chair and the wall, and pulls out two beers, tossing me one.

It's only been a few months since I've seen them, but it hits me how much they're starting to age. I really should visit more often.

"Congrats. I always wanted to own a business. Just never

worked out," he says, flashing me a smile. "Don't fuck it up."

"Yeah, thanks, dad. Once I get moved, I'll have two extra bedrooms. You and Mom will have to come and visit. I plan to put a pool table in the garage."

"We'll be there."

"How have you and Mom been doing?"

"I'm good. Your mom is as batty as an underground cavern, as usual."

He complains, but they have one of those rare relationships people dream about. They met in high school, married a few years after, and just celebrated their thirty-fifth wedding anniversary last year. "I meant your health. Any more problems?"

"Nah, healthy as a horse. Thanks to your mother's paranoia, though, I have to eat like a damned rabbit. One little heart attack..."

The small heart attack he suffered last year scared the hell out of all of us, and I'm glad Mom is making him stick to his diet. "That rabbit food stole some pounds from you. You look good."

"Yeah, I haven't been this light since I was your age." He eyes my slim build. "Don't know where you got your genes from. We did have a skinny mailman for a while."

"I heard that, you codger," Mom says, stepping into the room. "And that better be your only beer before dinner." She turns to me. "Bailey is going to walk down to the corner store with me. She needs some feminine items."

Shit. I forgot. I should be keeping track. I'll have Veronica show me how to count the days since I'm sure there's some female secret involved. I know they don't just start on the first of the month like a utility bill. "Thanks, mom."

As soon as the back door shuts, Dad turns to me. "Have you heard from that bitch you married at all?"

"Not a peep."

"Girl needs a mother."

Sighing, I sit back and take a few swallows of beer. "Not that kind of mother. It's been over five years. Bailey barely remembers her anymore."

Dad nods. "No mother beats a bad mother any day, but there are a lot of fish in the sea, son. Reel one in for your girl."

After considering it for a moment, I ask, "Can you keep a secret? Even from Mom?"

"Of course."

"I'm seeing someone, but things are kind of at a standstill. Her name is Veronica and she has a five-year-old son. We spend a lot of time together. The kids get along and Bailey loves her."

"Is the boy's father in the picture?"

"No, he doesn't see him. And he's a great kid. We just...neither of us is willing to take the risk."

He sits back, giving me the same scrutinizing look that has always made me weigh my words. "What risk?"

Is he kidding? "Both of our kids have had a parent abandon them. They need to know they're the most important thing to us. I need Bailey to know she always comes first, that she'll always have me."

"I don't see how seeing another woman would negate any of that. You stepped up from the beginning with Bailey. And you've sacrificed years of your life raising her alone, which is damned commendable, but it doesn't mean you have to be alone forever. What's your real worry?"

"The same as Veronica's. If we get together, then things fall apart, Bailey loses another female in her life, and Veronica's son loses another father figure."

"But both kids are fine with you dating?" His forehead crinkles.

"Ah...they don't know. They think we're friends. And Aiden is too young to pay much attention."

Dad gives me the same stare he's given me for years when he thinks I'm being stupid. One of the last times I remember seeing it was when I told him I was going to try to get Bailey's mother back, right after she ran off. "Let me get this straight. You two sneak around and see each other to keep it hidden from your kids, even though her son likes you, and Bailey likes Veronica?"

Running my hand through my hair, I sigh, "It's not that simple."

His scrutinizing gaze takes me right back to childhood. "Do you love her?"

"I'm afraid I'm getting there."

He huffs and leans forward, his eyes on mine. "Don't bullshit me, kid. *Do you love her*?"

"Yes, damn it."

"Does she feel the same?"

"I think so, but I don't know if she'd admit it."

"Then don't be a coward. Life's a risk, and kids learn that lesson too. Don't let the worthless bitch you married make you afraid to try again. Bailey is a smart kid. She can handle it."

"And if the kids get attached, then we break up after a year or even longer?" I snap, aggravated at the way he's breaking everything down.

He shrugs and pops open another beer, handing it to me. "Then you act like adults and let the kids visit the ex. They'd still benefit from it."

He makes it sound so simple and obvious.

Fuck, maybe it is.

"I'll give it some thought."

Leaning back, he nods. "You do that, but don't wait too long. I know the days can seem long sometimes, and so can the weeks, hell, even the months can drag, but the years, son, they fly."

The front door opens, and Bailey enters with my mom. I still see her as that smiley toddler, but she's a young woman now. "Yeah, I'm starting to realize that."

Throughout the rest of the visit, my father's words play in my head. I'm not sure whether I could convince Veronica to make a go of this, but more and more I think I'm going to try. A lot is going to change for us in the next few months, and I don't want to add stress to Bailey's life, but once we're settled in our new place, I'll talk to V.

Because my father is right. It all goes by so fast.

Chapter Nine

Veronica

It's been a long day. Aiden was running a low fever when he woke up this morning, so I didn't want to send him to preschool and get the other kids sick. He seems to be feeling fine now though, and his temp is back to normal. Kids are weird.

"I only have one more room, Ade. Do you want to come with me?"

"Yes!" He leaps up from the hotel lobby couch, where he's spent the morning watching cartoons. It's like I let him out of prison. There's nothing worse to a little boy than having to sit still.

He follows me through the breezeway, and I cross my fingers that this will be an easy room. We seemed to skip spring this year and went right into summer, with the thermometer climbing into the nineties and the humidity keeping pace. My shirt clings to me uncomfortably, and I think I've sweat through the panties I'm wearing. Gross.

Aiden bops along like it doesn't affect him, grinning as we go into the room. "Don't touch anything," I warn as usual.

While I strip the bed, he wanders into the bathroom. Maybe five seconds later, he comes running back out. "Mom! I think somebody needs an ambulance!"

Oh fuck. What did he just see? If some junkie has

overdosed in the bathroom and he walked in on it, I'll never forgive myself.

As soon as I step through the door to the bathroom, he cries, "Somebody lost their penis!"

Maybe finding a junkie would be better. A big flesh colored dildo is suction cupped to the wall of the shower, the head pointing up. The slit looks like an eye that's having a look around, and possibly judging my parenting.

A snort of laughter jumps from my throat as I have to speak a sentence I never thought I'd have to say. "Nobody lost a penis. It's fake."

Aiden reaches out a hand, and I pull him back. "Don't touch it! It's...dirty." I'm assuming, because thank fuck it isn't obviously used, but still, I doubt they stuck it there for a joke. Let's hope Aiden doesn't doubt it.

"Like Bill's fake leg?" His face screws up, and I know he's picturing someone with a prosthetic penis. I'm going to need a raise to pay for his therapy. I open my mouth to explain, but an excited smile jumps across his face. "Can I get a fake one? If I had two, I could sword fight them!" He starts jumping around, pretending to swing a sword.

"No, it's just a joke. Somebody thought it'd be funny to leave it there."

"A joke? Like my fake dog poo?"

"Yes, exactly like that."

"Oh." He stares at it for a moment. "Can I have it?"

"No, it's dirty and it's going in the trash as soon as I grab some gloves." Steering him out of the bathroom, I dig in my pocket and hand him a dollar. "Why don't you get a root beer from the vending machine? I'll be done here soon."

Distraction is my best bet right now.

"Okay!" He takes the money and races off.

The machine is right down the hall, and I peek out to watch him. Max joins him, chatting with him while they peruse the snack selection, so I know he's okay. All the rooms are empty so there's no stranger danger at the moment.

I grab my gloves and step back inside, shaking my head.

Menstrual cramps are trying to split me in half, I'm starving and sweating in places I didn't know had sweat glands, and my kid found a dildo I now have to dispose of. It's a safe bet the day can't get worse.

With plastic gloves in place, I reach for the monster that's been somewhere I don't want to think about, and tug, but it's really stuck onto the wall. I pull harder and it comes off with a pop and falls into the tub.

Ew. I've cleaned up a lot of gross stuff, but this is really skeeving me out. I quickly pick it up and chuck it into the trash bag, breathing a sigh of relief. When I return the trash bag to the cart, I check on Aiden, who is now sitting beside Max on the curb, eating a bag of chips and drinking his root beer. Max waves at me, and I mouth a thank you. I know he's keeping him entertained, though I can only imagine what Aiden is telling him.

The room isn't bad other than the disgusting sex toy, so it won't take me long. All I'm thinking about is a nice, cool shower, and the chocolate shake I plan to stop for on the way home when the ceiling seems to open up. Horrible smelling liquid rains down on me and the entire room, soaking me to the skin in seconds before I can even figure out what the hell is happening.

"Mom!" I look up to see Aiden standing just outside the doorway. "The fire alarm is ringing!"

"Stay right there!" I shout.

The sprinklers are still spraying and the water raining down has cleared, but not fast enough. Everything is covered in the sludgy, gray water that must've sat in those pipes for years. I don't smell smoke, but adrenaline kicks in anyway. Sprinklers don't go off unless there's a fire.

Aiden holds his nose when I rush out of the room. "Ugh, Mom, you smell like an egg fart."

Yeah, thanks for that, kid.

We rush down to the office, and every room we pass has water pouring out under the doors until we get to the front of the building, which seems to have been spared the rancid water treatment.

Jada, the clerk on duty today, bursts out laughing when I

step into the office, and clamps a hand over her mouth. "I'm sorry! I just. I'm sorry."

"What the hell is going on?"

"Something triggered the sprinklers in the back half of the building."

"Nothing is on fire?"

"No, Mike is looking into it now, but the fire department is on the way to double check." She grabs her purse and hands me my bag and keys. "We're all supposed to evacuate until they show up."

"Mom! A firetruck! Look!" Aiden shrieks, dancing around me as we step out into the sun baked parking lot.

"I see it. Let's wait over here, out of the way." We gather on the opposite side of the lot, under a tree since it's sweltering in the sun.

I'm grateful no one was hurt and that it isn't a real fire, but worry creeps in when I realize what this means. There's no way the hotel stays open while they're dealing with this. I don't know how much time this is going to put me out of work, but even a few days will hurt us.

Mike, the manager, approaches us, wiping at the back of his neck. "Veronica, Jada, you can go on home. I'll call you as soon as I know what our next step is."

"I'm sorry, Mike. I hope insurance covers everything," I tell him.

"Me too."

Jada wastes no time leaving, but I'm not going to get out of here without letting Aiden talk to a firefighter. It'd break his heart.

"Mom! They're going to leave! I want to see the truck up close!"

"Just for a minute, Ade. I'm all gross and I need a shower."

The fireman couldn't be nicer. They spend twenty minutes with Aiden, letting him check out the truck, beep the horn, and try on one of their heavy coats. He rushes up to me with one of the firefighters in tow, talking excitedly about everything he's learned. I'm only half listening, smelling like a dumpster is a bit distracting, until I hear him announce.

"And he said there wasn't a fire and it may have been a prank. A prank is like a joke, just like the fake penis we found in the tub." While I'm trying to look anywhere but at the handsome, grinning firefighter, Aiden goes on, oblivious to the fact I want to climb under the truck. "Hey! Maybe the same guy who left the joke penis played this joke too!"

The firefighter grins at me, and I shake my head with a sigh. "Thanks for taking the time to show him the truck and everything." I grab Aiden's hand. "Come on, we need to go. I need a shower."

"Bye Mr. Fireman!" Aiden cries, with a toothy smile.

"Bye Aiden! Be good for your mom." He winks at me. "She's had a rough day."

Two days pass before I hear from Mike, and fear streaks through me at his first words. "It'll take at least a month before we can open for business again. The water damage has also exposed some mold issues among other things, so I've decided to close for a month while repairs are being made."

A month of no income.

A month, at least.

"Veronica, are you there?"

"Yeah." I swallow and flop onto the couch. "I'm here. I'm sorry to hear that. At least the insurance is picking up the tab."

"Yeah, and as long as we have to shut down anyway, I'm going to get some remodeling done that I've been meaning to do for years. Which is why I need to ask a favor of you."

"Okay."

"I'd like to take my family on a vacation. It's been years since we've been able to get away. Max will be overseeing the work and keeping in touch with me, but I'd like to have someone here full time. Just to keep up the lobby and the few unaffected rooms, keep an eye on the place at night, set the alarm, etc. Suite one hundred wasn't damaged, so I wanted to see if you would be willing to live here for the next two weeks. I know it'll be a pain in the ass since you have a young kid, and there may be a day or two that they shut off the water, but I'll pay you double your monthly salary to stay for two weeks."

Is he kidding? Two months of pay just to stay there and keep an eye on the place? "Sure, Mike, I can do that. When do you want to leave?" I reply, trying not to sound as relieved as I am. This could easily have been the phone call that meant I would be job hunting.

"Tomorrow if that's not too soon. Around noon?"

"I'll be there."

"Oh, and the pool wasn't damaged. Max will keep up with the maintenance so you'll have something to do while you're here."

"Sounds good. Aiden will be thrilled."

"Thanks, Veronica. I'll fill you in on the little stuff when you get here."

I guess we're spending two weeks at the hotel.

If Neal presses his lips together any harder, they're going to disappear. I'm not sure exactly what's causing this reaction, but I don't have time to argue with him.

"This is crazy. You'll be alone in a hotel for two weeks? What if someone tries to break in? Especially if it's under construction! People rob construction sites all the time!"

Aiden and Bailey's giggles filter in through the window as they throw a frisbee just outside, and I take a quick peek to make sure Aiden didn't overhear. "Would you keep it down? I don't want Aiden to be afraid to stay there, and there's an alarm that I'll set every night. And a police precinct three blocks away so it wouldn't take long if we needed help."

What I won't admit is that it does make me a bit nervous. Working this job has taught me that people are crazy. I'm likely going to have to deal with irate customers insisting on a room no matter what shape the hotel is in. And he's not wrong about construction sites being a common target for burglars.

I shove Aiden's swim shorts into his suitcase and zip it closed, moving to finish packing mine.

"You'll still be alone."

"Aiden will be with me."

My grin is met with a glare before he crosses his arms and announces, "I'm staying with you."

What?

"Excuse me?"

"It's an empty hotel. I'm sure you can find a room for Bailey and me. We'll stay with you."

"I—" I bite my lip to restrain myself from arguing. The truth is I'd love to have them there. Our suite has an adjoining room with two beds and I'm sure we could sneak in some happy naked times while the kids are asleep. "I'll have to ask the owner."

"If he doesn't like it, he can talk to me."

Sighing, I turn around away to shove my clothes into my suitcase. "Lose the caveman act, Neal. I'm not in the mood to deal with any alpha male bullshit." I've already had to deal with Aiden's tantrum over not wanting to go. I understand why he doesn't want to stay there, but we need the money. There's no help for it.

Strong arms wrap around my waist and his body presses against my back. Resting his chin on my shoulder, he murmurs in my ear. "I'll show you my caveman side when I drag you off to one of the other rooms once the kids are asleep."

My body goes limp and I tilt my head, giving him more access as he plants kisses up my neck. "Are you trying to bribe me with sex?"

I can feel his smile against my skin. "Is it working?"

"I don't know. I might need to hear more."

His hands travel up to massage my breasts, his lips continuing their path up my neck. God, this man knows how to make me melt in seconds. I don't know whether to be impressed or terrified at the way he makes my body respond to him.

"More, huh? Like how I'm going to lick you until you can't take anymore? Is that what you want to hear? Or how I'm going to lay you on your stomach, your ass in the air, and take you from behind."

Fuck me I never had a chance.

The sound of the front door opening makes him step back, and I try to continue packing like I'm not a pile of hormones that just wants to ride him like a bumper car, so he can slam into me over and over.

"Let me make a call."

Mike is fine with them staying as well. In fact, he sounds happy with the idea so maybe he wasn't completely comfortable having us there alone either. "As long as the place is in good shape when I return, I don't care what friends you have with you," he tells me. "Just don't let anyone drown in the pool or get hurt."

"Thanks, Mike. We'll be there by noon." Hanging up the phone, I turn and smile at Neal, all the dirty possibilities running through my head. "Go get packed."

The suite we're staying in is the nicest in the hotel and was unaffected by the sprinklers. It includes two bedrooms, a sitting area with a sofa and TV, a tiny kitchen with a microwave, toaster oven, refrigerator, and sink, and a large bathroom with a sunken tub big enough for four people.

A door which can be locked on both sides separates the suite from an adjoining room that was also spared from the damage. It has two beds, a small sofa, TV, and attached bathroom. As Neal places his bag on the bed, Bailey announces, "This is mine and Aiden's room!"

"Yes!" Aiden darts inside and dives on the bed closest to the wall. "I want this bed!"

Neal looks at me, his eyebrows climbing his forehead. We planned for him and Bailey to stay in this room and he could sneak into the suite at night.

Shrugging, I put Aiden's suitcase on the bed and start moving his clothes to the drawers. "The suite has two bedrooms.

I suppose I could put up with you snoring in the other room."

Neal flashes me a wicked smile before he goes to inspect the door which leads out to the parking lot. "Okay, but I want this door to stay locked all the time. Just like this. You understand?" He directs his words toward Bailey, and she nods. "Aiden, do you promise not to unlock this door? Only go in and out through your Mom's room?"

"I promise!"

The outer door has a lock on the knob, a deadbolt, and a swing bar guard at the top instead of a chain. There's no danger of anyone getting in, and we'll be on the other side of the wall, so I guess it would be okay for the kids to stay in this adjoining room.

"Can we go swimming?" Aiden asks, bouncing up and down.

"Let me get a few things unpacked, Ade. And that's another thing." I kneel down in front of him, so I can be sure he's looking at me and listening. "You don't go near the pool without either me or Neal with you. Not even one step inside the fence. Do you understand?"

"Yes."

"I mean it. If you're inside the fence without us, you won't be swimming again while we're here."

"I won't! I promise!"

Neal cautions Bailey as well. "I know you're a good swimmer, but you never know what could happen."

Once we're convinced both kids know the rules, we spend the next few minutes unpacking and getting settled in. Both kids are dying to get in the pool, so we head outside. We really do have it made while we're here. No bills to pay, no other people to bother us, and an entire swimming pool to ourselves. I'm sure the kids will get bored faster than we will, but for now, they're thrilled.

I drag four chairs together by the shallow end of the pool and toss a towel on each one. "Aiden!" I call as he starts to dart away. "Sunscreen!"

Aiden and then Bailey stand still while I spray them down, then they jump into the water. I dig into my bag to find the book I've been reading and spread out on my stomach to soak in the sun and read.

I peek up after a few minutes to see Neal looking at me. "What are you looking at?"

"You're lying on your stomach in a bikini. What do you think I'm looking at?" His tongue darts out to wet his lips, and I don't know if it was an unconscious action or deliberate, but it doesn't matter because its effect on me is the same.

Glancing toward the pool, I make sure the kids are out of earshot. They're playing Marco Polo, so they can't hear. "You know what I've been thinking about all day?"

"Me?" he teases.

"Well, sort of. I've been thinking about how you grit your teeth and hiss when I blow you. I'd really like to do that tonight."

His mouth falls open and he takes a deep breath. "Fuck, V, you can't tell me that in the middle of the afternoon. I'm going to be hard until tonight."

I can't help myself. I've never had a guy that seems to get worked up over me the way Neal does. Rolling over, I tuck my hands behind my head, making my breasts push against the thin material of my bikini. My nipples could key a car right now and it doesn't escape his attention. I grab my spray bottle and mist my neck and chest. "Ah, that's better. So, is that a no, then?"

His lip quirks up and he sits upright. "Keep teasing me, woman, and see what happens." He grabs a tube of sunblock and scoots his chair closer to mine. "You look a little red. Let me help you."

He's positioned where the kids can't see exactly what he's doing, since his back is toward them, plus they're caught up in their own fun.

The cold lotion makes me gasp when his hands land on my ankle, but it warms quickly. His hands feel amazing as they rub and massage much longer than necessary to spread the lotion, working their way slowly up my leg. His fingers barely brush over my crotch, just enough to drive me crazy, before he moves back and starts at the other ankle, giving my other leg the same treatment.

I shouldn't have started this. He's way better at tormenting me. And dark has never seemed so far away.

"You okay?" he asks, and I want to kiss his taunting smile.

"I'm good." Sure, just ignore the fact my voice is way too high.

"Turn over, let me get your back."

A glance at the pool shows me the kids are playing with innertubes, taking turns jumping into them. As soon as I roll over, he smacks my ass. "Neal! The kids!"

"Are completely ignoring us." He sits on the edge of my chair, and I let out a groan when his hands start kneading my shoulders. Slowly, he works his way down to my lower back leaving me in a puddle on the chair. Leaning over, he murmurs in my ear. "You can suck me all you want tonight, but you're still going to end up with your ass in the air, trying not to scream while I fuck you."

Dead.

I'm dead.

He wins.

"No fair. I'm no good at dirty talk."

He chuckles and squeezes my ass before retreating back to his chair. "But you like it."

"From you, yeah."

His eyes squint at the edges as he smiles at me. "You can talk dirty. Anyone can."

"Nope, I'm terrible at it."

"We'll see."

The kids run up, and Aiden flops down beside me, dripping cold water down my back. "I'm hungry."

"Me too," Bailey adds. "Can we order a pizza for dinner?"

Neal glances at me and shrugs. "Sounds good to me."

My phone rings, and I get a strange look from Neal and Bailey when they hear my ringtone. What can I say? The wicked witch music from The Wizard of Oz is perfect for my mother's tone.

Neal snorts out a laugh when I say, "Shit. It's my mother. I need to take this."

"Come on," he tells the kids. "You guys can get showered

while I order some food."

I mouth a thank you before accepting the call I know is going to make me do something I don't want to do.

Chapter Ten

Neal

While the kids are hogging the bathrooms, taking their showers, I watch Veronica through the window. She paces back and forth around the pool while she talks, her face reflecting her annoyance. Finally, she hangs up, sits down on the chair, and flops back, rubbing her forehead. I hope she didn't get bad news.

By the time I've ordered our dinner and made sure Aiden is dressed, I hear her come back into the suite. Aiden curls up on the bed to watch cartoons, and Bailey stretches out on the other bed to read, so I head over to the suite to wait for the pizza.

"Hey," she says, a smile pushing across her face. "Do you want the next shower?"

"Nah, go ahead. I don't have sunblock to shower off. When you have the golden skin of a god, you don't need it."

She snorts and shakes her head, grabbing a change of clothes.

"Is everything okay?"

I don't want to push her if she doesn't want to talk, but she's also not the type to just volunteer information, especially if it's negative.

"Yeah, just my mom and her bullshit. I'll tell you about it later, okay?"

She heads into the bathroom, and I hear the shower start up. The urge to join her is only slightly less than the fear of one of the kids wandering over, plus I have to wait for our food. It's killing me that she's all naked and soapy on the other side of the wall.

With a sigh, I sit at the table by the window and prop my feet up on the opposite chair. I wonder what her mother said that riled her up. She doesn't really talk about her parents. I mean, I know she never knew her father, that he bailed before she was born, but her mother lives nearby. It's a little odd in all the time we've spent together that I've never seen her. She's never come by, not even to pick up her grandkid. There must be some kind of family drama.

"Neal! Grab me a towel from the drawer. The kids took them all," Veronica calls out.

"Come on out and get one. The kids are in the other room," I tease.

"Don't be an ass!"

"Okay. Hang on."

I get to my feet just as there's a knock at the door. Assuming it's the pizza guy, I call out while I'm opening the drawers, trying to find a towel, "Come on in!"

The door opens, spilling the late afternoon light across the floor. "The money is on the table," I tell him, absently. It takes a second before I realize the room is dead silent, but it doesn't stay that way. A squeal echoes through the room, and I look up to see Veronica streak back toward the bathroom, her naked ass glistening and jiggling, while a young guy stands frozen in the doorway, his eyebrows touching his hairline.

"Uh—yeah, sorry," he mumbles. "I thought I heard you tell me to come in." He snatches the money off of the table and puts the boxes in its place.

"I did," I reply, trying not to laugh as a string of curses spills from the bathroom. Most include shoving something into one of my orifices not designed for such use. The kid can't be more than seventeen and his face is growing redder by the second. "I'm sorry. Keep the change."

As soon as the door shuts behind him, I step into the bathroom and hold out a towel. Veronica sits on the edge of the tub, glaring at me. "You told me the kids weren't there and to come on in!"

"No, I told the pizza guy to come in and you to hang on a second." A laugh jumps from my throat. "It was a misunderstanding."

"Stop laughing at me!" She throws a wet washcloth at me and it slaps against my chest before hitting the floor. "I probably scarred the kid for life."

"I'm not laughing." My guts are about to burst from holding it in, though. "And you made his day." My eyes are pulled down to the bare patch between her legs. "When did you start shaving?"

"I'm going to shave your balls in your sleep if you don't wipe that smile off your face. Get out of here before the kids see us."

The twitch of her lips assures me she's not really mad, but I can't wait to tease her about this later.

The kids eat at the table in their room where they can watch cartoons, which gives Veronica and I a little time alone. I'm trying to find a way to ask her about the call from her mother in a way that won't sound nosy when she asks, "Do you think you could keep Aiden for a few hours tomorrow? I need to help my mom with something. Max will be here overseeing the work crew until around six, and I'll be back before then, so you wouldn't need to do anything other than entertain the kids."

"I don't mind watching Aiden. What's going on with your mom?"

"Nothing out of the ordinary," she grumbles, taking a bite of her bread stick.

"You never talk about her. She lives locally, right?"

"Out in the county, about thirty minutes from here. We aren't close or anything, but I'm her first call if something goes wrong." She pauses long enough for me to think that's all the information she's willing to share, but then continues. "The board of health is threatening her with fines if she doesn't clean up the property a little and cut the grass. It hasn't been cut at all this year so it's probably waist high in some areas. I just need to go out and cut the area around her house and down to the road. They'll leave her alone."

"Does she live alone?"

"Her ex lives in another trailer on the property and he was keeping up with it, at least enough to keep the board of health off her back, but he broke his leg and can't do it right now."

I have a ton of questions, but I'll save them because her clipped tone tells me she isn't thrilled about this conversation. "I'll go with you. You can hang out with your mom and the kids while I cut the grass."

"No." The word flies from her mouth whip fast. A second later she says, "Sorry, I don't mean to snap at you, but you don't know what you're getting yourself into. It's going to be a damn jungle."

"I'll borrow George's field and brush mower. It goes through anything."

Sighing, she sits back and wipes her mouth with a paper napkin. "It's not just grass. I don't take anyone out there, Neal. It's disgusting. Her and her ex are both hoarders. Her house is stuffed full and trust me, you wouldn't want Bailey in there. It isn't safe."

Her face flushes, and I reach across to grab her hand. "V, you don't have to be embarrassed. I swear I won't judge. We can't control what our parents do."

She's quiet for a moment, and I give her time to think. "The field and brush mower would probably make the job quick. There's a nice little creek on the property. I could take them there to play, I suppose."

"Good."

Her gaze meets mine. "It wasn't that bad when I lived at home. I mean, it was bad, and I couldn't wait to get out, but not like it is now. I'm not…dirty like that."

I get up and pull her to her feet and into a hug she really looks like she needs. Veronica is always so happy, peppy, and quick witted. She doesn't display this vulnerable side very often and I want her to know she can. "I would never think that. Your place is always spotless. If anything, you're a bit of a clean freak."

And now I understand why.

"It'll be fine. Let me help. This is what we do, remember? We help each other. I cut your mom's grass, you have the sex talk with my daughter, quid pro quo." Yeah, I threw that in there. I've been trying to find a way to bring it up.

Laughing, she steps back. "You want me to tell Bailey about sex? I hate to break it to you, buddy, but she probably already knows. By her age, her friends have spread the word."

Groaning, I sit back down. "Maybe, but she needs to know everything. I'm sure she has questions. I was hoping my sister would step in, but Bailey doesn't trust her the way she does you."

"Of course I'll talk to her. So, should I start with blow jobs or lube or—"

"Stop!" I cover my ears and put my head down. Her laughter makes me smile, and when I look up again, Bailey is walking toward us.

"Why were you covering your ears?"

"Because he's a big baby who can't stand hearing about woman things like epithelial linings," Veronica says, and they both break into laughter.

"Very funny. Is Aiden finished eating?" Definitely time to change the subject.

"Yeah, but he's falling asleep. I thought you might not want him to."

Veronica is on her feet. "Oh hell no. If he takes a nap this late, he'll never sleep tonight."

Bailey grins at me. "Can I go outside and ride my bike in the parking lot? I'm bored."

"Sure, no need to get salty, brah, I'll sit out with you." I get the usual eye roll from Bailey, but I hear Veronica giggle from the next room.

By the time Veronica has dragged a whiny Aiden outside, I've pulled the kids bikes off the rear rack of my car and Bailey is happily circling the lot. Aiden perks up when he sees his, and Veronica barely has time to strap the helmet on his head before he's off, following Bailey.

Veronica grabs two folding chairs from her trunk and we sit down under the tree to watch them. "He's ready for the training wheels to come off," I observe, watching the way he controls the bike.

"Yeah, I just haven't made the time to teach him yet."

"I can show him this week."

Veronica smiles, watching the kids play. "That'd be great. He won't whine as much when he gets hurt if you teach him. He has to keep up the tough guy act, you know."

"It's not an act. Males are tougher. It's just a fact," I tease.

"Says the man who was going to take his daughter to the emergency room for a period."

Grinning at her, I shake my head. "Touche."

"We should take a cooler with some drinks and sandwiches with us tomorrow. We need to keep the kids out of her house. I have a bag cooler that will work."

"Does she have running water? A working bathroom?"

"Yeah, but they'd be better off pissing in the woods."

Christ. "That bad, huh?"

"You'll see," she sighs.

It's not that I don't believe her, but everyone is a bit embarrassed of their parents and where they come from. It's probably not as bad as she makes it sound.

It's worse.

Oh god, so much worse.

As soon as we pull into the driveway of Veronica's mother's house, I know this isn't going to be any quick job. It's a good thing George loaned me his mower because no normal riding mower would have made it through this.

Not to mention, I'd have to keep getting off to move stuff, like the two toilets sitting in the field, surrounded by rotting wooden pallets.

"Listen, guys," Veronica says to the kids, before they can climb out of the back seat. "I know I already explained once, but I want to make sure you remember. If she asks if you'd like something to drink or eat, the answer is no. I have food in the cooler. I don't care what it is, it could make you sick. She never checks expiration dates. We're just going to say hi, and let Neal get started, then I'll take you into the woods to play in the creek."

"I want to try to build a dam," Bailey says, helping Aiden out of the car.

"You can't say that!" His mouth drops open. "Neal! She's cursing!"

"Ade, don't be a tattletale. And she's talking about a big wall that holds back water. That kind of dam isn't cursing," Veronica admonishes.

Aiden stops in his tracks. "So, I can say it?" A grin spreads across his face and he whispers. "Dam."

Bailey giggles as he continues.

"We can build a dam. Dam dam, we'll build a dam dam." He dances around, singing his dam song, and Veronica turns away to hide a grin.

"I think that's enough," she says, as a woman opens the front door of the house and steps onto the porch. Well, she walks through the narrow path carved out between piles of junk and down the steps. Veronica must take after her absent father, because there's not much resemblance, other than the red hair.

"I didn't know you were bringing company," she says, watching us like we might make off with some of the crap piled around us. Are those toasters? Who needs four toasters and why are they on the edge of the porch in a rusting heap?

"Mom, this is my friend, Neal, and his daughter, Bailey. Neal is going to cut the grass while I take the kids back to play in the creek." She turns to us. "This is my mother, Patty."

"It's nice to meet you, Patty," Neal says.

"I'm going to build a dam!" Aiden announces. "It'll be the best damn dam that ever…dammed!"

"Aiden!" Veronica snaps. "Enough!"

"Well, come on in and cool down before you get started. It's hot out here."

"Thanks, but Neal needs to get started. We have some other stuff to do this evening," she lies. "I have a picnic lunch packed if you'd like to join us at the creek."

"In this heat? You must be soft headed. You guys go on and do your thing. I'm going to check on Marvin. Let him know what's going on."

With that said, she hurries down the steps and across the drive toward the dilapidated trailer on the far side of the driveway. She must go back and forth a lot, because there's a path between them.

"Nice seeing you," Veronica mumbles. She forces a smile and turns to the kids. "Okay, let me show Neal where the shed is, and we'll go play. Stay on the path. With the grass this high, there could be a snake and you don't want to step on it."

As we make our way behind the house to a surprisingly new and shiny shed, Bailey starts teaching Aiden about snakes. "There are a lot of species who live in our area and most are harmless, but we do have copperheads and if we're close to water, probably cottonmouths."

"They have cotton in their mouths?" I look behind us to see he's taken her hand.

"No, they're called that because the inside of their mouths are white, like cotton."

"Oh." It's cute and funny the way he responds to her. Anything out of Bailey's mouth is gospel.

Veronica pulls open the shed to reveal a riding mower, weed eater, and an assortment of tools and trimmers. "Whatever you need, I'm sure they have five of them," she says. "And there's gasoline in those cans." She points to a few gas cans in the corner.

The air in the shed is too hot to breathe for more than a minute or two. This is crazy. "You can't store gas like that! It could explode and set the whole place on fire."

She lets out a humorless laugh. "They have set the woods on fire twice...in the last year. This is a compromise because the last time I visited, there were gas and kerosene cans in the house. Better to blow up the shed."

That is insane.

She turns to me. “It’s not too late to change your mind. I told you it’d be terrible.”

And let her do it? Yeah, that’ll happen. “No way. I’ve got this.”

“Okay, well, only do the front yard and along the edge of the road. That’s what the county is complaining about. The fields are so full of trash you’d tear up any mower you tried to use anyway.”

“How much land do they have?”

Veronica gestures to the tree line. “Almost two hundred acres. This place was a working farm back in it’s day, and the back field was an apple orchard. The trees still bear occasionally, but it’s so trashed and overgrown, they just fall and rot with the other garbage.” She points to a narrow path in the woods. “That path leads down to the creek. It’s only about a quarter of a mile. If you come looking for us.”

The kids start down the path, and Bailey stops by a tree where we can still see them.

Veronica hesitates and shifts the backpack cooler she’s wearing. “I hate this. This isn’t your job. I should at least be helping.”

“Psh. This is one of those manly jobs. You need my masculine muscles and strength. Now, you go make sure the kids don’t drown, and I’ll get all nice and sweaty for you.”

“Yeah, man stink really turns me on. You know me so well.”

“It’s a gift.”

“Uh-huh.” She smiles up at me. “Trust me, swamp ass will not make up for your stellar pelvic acumen.”

“Come on, Mom!” Aiden yells. “Dam!”

We both break into laughter, and she shakes her head. “Okay, call me when you’re done or come find us.”

What the hell have I gotten myself into? I intended to cut the yard and at least the front field, but a quick walk through it shows me Veronica was right. I can’t go five steps without running into a hunk of rusted metal, or an old garden hose, or…is that a vehicle transmission? It's like the saying, everything but the kitchen sink. No, there's a sink, lying on its side, full of stagnant water, a cloud of bugs swarming above it. I'm glad we thought to spray ourselves down with bug repellent before we came.

I settle for running the massive field and brush mower through the front yard, along the edges of the road, and making a clear path to the mailbox, shed, and driveway. Even with the super powered mower, it takes me nearly three hours. My sweat slickened skin is covered with bits of cut grass, pollen, and god knows what else.

By the time I'm finished, that creek sounds pretty good.

The hike is easy, and I can hear the kids before I see them. As I step through the trees, Veronica comes into view. She's reclining on a large boulder at the edge of the creek, leaning back on her hands, her feet dangling in the fast running water. The sun slants through the trees, turning her hair to fire and making her pale skin glisten.

"Hey!" she calls, finally noticing that I'm staring at her like a lovestruck idiot. "Are you done?"

"Yeah, it's the best I can do under the circumstances." I think we need to get out here and try to clean some of this up for her mother. She obviously isn't able and a few weekends with the right equipment, and a couple of dumpsters would make a world of difference.

I wade into the creek, find a spot deep enough to submerge myself completely, and wash off the sweat and grit. Her gaze is locked on me when I look up and the hungry look in her eyes makes me want to strip her right here.

Damn kids.

"Hungry?" she asks, offering me a sandwich from the cooler bag.

"Starving." She scoots over a bit as I sit beside her and take the sandwich. "How long has the property been like this?"

"As long as I can remember. It gets steadily worse as they buy more and more crap just to eventually add it to the pile."

"We should help. I could get a couple of guys out here, and

it wouldn't take too long."

Sighing, she shakes her head, kicking her feet in the cool water. "She'd never let you. She's a hoarder. You haven't seen the worst of it."

"If we just removed the trash in the yard and fields, they could be cut—"

She puts a hand on my arm. "You don't understand. To her and Marvin, none of it is trash. Nothing is trash. If you brought a dumpster out here, she'd call the police and have you removed."

She can't be serious.

"Even the toilets? The pile of rotting pallets? There's an old vacuum cleaner lying in the field."

"Believe me, Neal, I've tried. About five years ago, she spent a few days visiting relatives, and I took the opportunity to try to clean up. When she got home, she lost her shit, screaming and cursing, because I threw away her 'stuff'. Trash service wasn't scheduled to pick up until the next day so she spent the night digging through the cans, returning everything to where it was. And adding to her collections."

Aiden screeches, and Bailey giggles as they try to catch a frog, and we get hit with a mist of water from their splashing around.

"Collections?"

"Her house and every outbuilding on this property are stuffed full. Of trash. She has one whole building full of empty potato chip cans and tissue boxes. And trust me, if the place was on fire, she'd save those before any of us. I appreciate that you want to help, but you've done what you can do."

Her voice is getting tense, and I get it. I'd be embarrassed too, if this is how I grew up. "Okay, then." I polish off the sandwich. "Ready to go?"

The kids complain about leaving, but it's clear on the hike back that they're getting tired. Veronica's mother sticks her head out the door and shouts a thank you as we get ready to leave, then retreats back inside.

My heart goes out to Veronica and Aiden. Anytime I visit my parents, they can't get enough of Bailey, and I feel bad that they don't see her enough. Yet, here is one of Aiden's grandparents who lives so close and has no interest. Doesn't even come out to give him a hug or anything. It pisses me off.

Considering Aiden's father has nothing to do with him, Veronica and Aiden only have each other.

After we get back to the hotel, the kids get cleaned up and rest for a bit in their room. Veronica comes up behind me and snakes her arms around my waist. "Mike keeps a grill out back. I'm sure he wouldn't mind if we used it."

"Sounds good to me."

"I'll run over to the grocery store while you fire it up." She steps back and turns to call for Aiden, but I plant a quick kiss on her lips. "Leave him here. He's fine."

"Okay."

The grill is in pretty good shape, and there's charcoal handy as well, so I drag the setup around to the front and light the coals. While it burns down, I take a seat in one of the two chairs under the tree and Aiden wanders over to join me.

"Hey, buddy. Where is Bailey?"

"Watching some stupid girly cartoon with ponies." He plops down in the dirt and starts digging around with a stick. "Why is the dirt in little piles?"

"Because groundhogs have been here. They build tunnels underground."

"Oh, cool." He's quiet for a moment before asking the last question I expected and one I'm not equipped to deal with. "Neal? Where do women get babies from? Bailey won't tell me. She said to ask you."

Thank you, Bailey. I just asked Veronica to have this talk with her, and there's no way I'm explaining this to a five year old. I don't know what to tell a kid this age. The stork? Birds and bees? Panicking, I blurt. "From underground."

He looks up at me, his eyes wide and his nose crinkled up. "Underground? Like the groundhogs?"

Sure. Why not. Sounds as plausible as a stork. "Yeah, you have to catch a baby groundhog, bring it inside to live with you, and feed it people food."

"And it turns into a baby," he says, nodding with a grin.

Something tells me I'm going to be in trouble for this one. "A, do you want to learn to ride your bike without the training wheels?" I ask.

The distraction works, and he jumps to his feet. "Yes! Mom won't let me take them off."

"She won't mind. Bring your bike over here."

When Veronica returns, she and Bailey sit under the tree, watching as Aiden tries, falls, and gets back on, so determined. Finally, he makes it a few wobbly yards before crashing into the grassy embankment. "I did it!" he cries, running to me. I grab him and swing him up into a hug. "Yes, you did!" He peeks over my shoulder. "Mom! Did you see?"

Veronica beams at him, but I swear she looks like she could cry. "I saw. You did awesome!" He rushes over to get a high five from Bailey.

I return to the grill that's now ready to use and get dinner started. Veronica sits under the tree, watching the kids run and play.

I save this moment, like a snapshot in time, because for some reason, it feels so right. I realize what I'm feeling isn't just happiness, but contentment. I'm right where I want to be with the people I want to be with.

It doesn't get better than this.

My thoughts are interrupted when Veronica walks up, a smirk on her face. "Neal, why is my kid trying to find a baby groundhog to feed?"

Shrugging, I hand her the plate of chicken. "He wants a brother."

Chapter Eleven

Neal

It's Veronica's last night at the hotel. Though I went back to work a few days ago, I've still been staying with her at night. Bailey was happy to stay at the hotel instead of being dragged to the car wash with me. Once we live right across the street, she'll be able to stay home alone while I work, and I know she's looking forward to that.

The last two weeks have flown by. We've spent a lot of time with the kids, playing, swimming, and enjoying the summer weather. Since it's our last night, we've done our best to exhaust the kids today in hopes they won't interrupt us tonight. It seems to have worked because they're both sound asleep early, and I quietly latch the lock on the door between our rooms. We always unlock it after, before heading to separate beds so they don't see us together in the morning.

I've been working Veronica up all day by saying dirty things to her whenever I had the chance. I can't help myself. I love how turned on she gets from it. I've also been teasing her about talking dirty to me. It's not really that I'm all that into it, but I want her to relax and not be embarrassed to talk to me that way.

She comes out of the bathroom wearing only panties and a camisole, and my body instantly responds. "What?" she says, grabbing a brush and running it through her hair. She's so innocent in some ways. Any other woman, I'd think they were playing coy, but she really has no idea how beautiful she is or what the sight of her does to me.

"Just thinking about how tight you're going to wrap those legs around me when I eat your pussy."

Her chest rises and falls, and she shakes her head, looking away with a grin. I catch her off guard, coming up behind her before she can turn back around. Her small body is warm against my chest when I wrap an arm around her, pulling her back against me. Her skin smells like the cherry body wash she favors, and I lick at the scent on her neck. "Don't even try to act like you don't like my dirty talk." My finger flicks over her hard nipple. "Your body gives you away."

"I do like it," she murmurs, tilting her head back.

"Have you been thinking about the dirty things you want to say to me tonight?" My hands wander to her waistband, hooking inside and pulling them down.

"Like mud puddles and the soles of shoes," she giggles.

"Not even close."

Her eyes close, and she groans when I slide a finger between her legs. Already wet. Perfect.

"I can't talk dirty. It'll sound stupid," she breathes.

"Not to me," I promise. "Now, get your sexy ass in the bed because we have one night left here and every second I'm not inside of you is a waste."

After the buildup and teasing all day, we're both ravenous for each other, and I barely have her in the bed before I'm sliding inside of her. It's like a switch is flipped and she becomes the insatiable, passionate lover that rests just behind that youthful innocence.

She gasps and whimpers through her first orgasm, trying not to wake the kids, then grins up at me and rolls us over so she's on top. She's gorgeous like this. Wild hair stuck to damp skin, perky tits thrust out as she teases me, grinding against me without actually letting me inside. Now is the time. "Such a tease. Talk to me, V. You can do it. Call me names, whatever you want. Anything goes."

Biting her lip, her cheeks flush and she grinds against me. "Does that feel good?" she says, testing the waters.

"So good. Tell me what you're going to do."

"I'm going to drive you crazy, then fuck you until you…come inside me," she says, faltering a little at the end. She's getting the hang of it now.

She grabs my cock and guides it in, a satisfied grin on her face when I groan, "Fuuuuck, yes."

I'll never forget the next words out of her mouth as she fucks me. Gaining confidence, she thrusts her hips and says, "Yeah, feels good, doesn't it you…fucking idiot."

It takes a second for it to register, but I can't help my response. My chest nearly bursts with restrained laughter that only manages a few seconds before erupting. Her face turns bright red, and I feel bad, but I can't stop laughing. She called me a fucking idiot. To turn me on. Priceless.

"I told you!" she exclaims, slapping my chest. "I'm not saying anything else!"

She starts to get off me. Still chuckling, I roll us over and thrust into her hard and fast. "Neal! God!" she cries out, her hands clawing my ass.

In less than a minute, I feel her pulse around me and let myself go. It's got to be the first time I've gotten off while fighting the urge to laugh. Leave it to this crazy girl to give me a new experience when I was attempting to get her outside of her comfort zone.

"Neal," she whispers, rolling over and pulling a pillow over to her.

"Hmm?" I kiss down her back and pull the covers up over us.

"We will never speak of this again."

A snort of laughter leaps out of me. "You mean the fact I made you come so fast, or that you think I'm a fucking idiot?"

"Both seem like excellent topics to avoid."

"You're adorable."

"I hate you."

"Not even close, sweetheart."

"We have four whole hours," Veronica emphasizes. "I told Aiden's teacher I'd pick him up at three. There's no reason for him to stay late when I'm not working."

"Bailey won't be back until five. My sister is taking her to some spa for a girl's day."

Veronica leans against the kitchen counter. Ever since the night I got her naked against the wall in here, it's all I can think about when I walk into this room. "So I can take my time with you," she says. Her expression turns impish. "How open minded are you?"

A tendril of red hair hangs free of her ponytail, and I tug on it. "Do you have something kinky in mind?"

She shrugs and opens the fridge. "It's pretty low on the kinky scale. Probably a two."

"You have a kinky scale? What's a ten?" I grab my bottle of water. Something tells me I'm going to need to be hydrated.

Her head pops over the fridge door, and she wears a wicked smile. "Me fucking you with a strap on."

It feels like none of the water I just took a swig of actually goes down the right pipe. Choking, I do my best not to spray it all over her floor. "What the hell?"

"What? I saw it in a porno. It looked kind of hot."

I don't know if she's screwing with me or serious, but we're going to get something straight. "Nothing goes in my ass. If anyone is taking it in the south mouth, it's you." I shake my head and grin at her. "You can't talk dirty during sex, but you can discuss strap-ons?"

"It's different." She steps back holding a can of whipped cream and bottle of chocolate sauce. "Now I want to make myself a cock sundae."

"I do already have the nuts."

Throwing an expectant glance back over her shoulder, she heads to the bedroom. By the time I've drained the bottle of water and followed her, she has covered the bed in a beach towel, and stands beside it, stark naked. I love that she is so comfortable with her body. I've hooked up with women years older than her who spend so much time trying to cover up and hide perceived flaws, no matter how much I assure them they're beautiful.

Veronica has no problem being nude. I don't think she realizes how amazing that is. It's not like she flounces around, showing off, she just doesn't shrink away from showering together or lounging naked with me once we're done. Her confidence is sexy as fuck.

"Okay, lose the clothes and lie down."

Her little bossy act is adorable. She's usually submissive in the bedroom, which I also love about her, but there's no way I'm passing up one of her long, slow blow jobs, so I'm perfectly fine following directions this time.

Shucking off my pants and underwear together, I hop on the bed, fold my arms behind my head, and grin up at her. "At your service."

She smiles at me, her gaze slowly sliding down my bare chest to my cock, that's ready and waiting. "Wow, that was fast. It's a wonder it didn't make a noise when it popped up."

Grinning, I ask, "What kind of noise?"

She crawls over me, straddling my thighs and shaking the bottle of chocolate sauce. "Maybe like boing? Did you ever play with those springy door stoppers when you were a kid?"

Laughter shakes my chest. I've never had so much fun with a woman, especially during sex. Is there any adult who can't instantly recall that sound? It seems to be a shared childhood memory for a few generations. "I'll never get that out of my head now."

My breath catches when she squirts the chocolate syrup on the head of my cock. Cold rivulets run down to my balls, but she adds some chocolate to them too. The feeling of it running down my ass crack doesn't scream sexy, but I'm not complaining. Leaning over, she gives the head of my cock a single lick before grabbing the whipped cream. By the time she's done, I can't see anything but chocolate and whipped cream. It's going to take her forever to lick all that off.

Awesome.

She adds a few finishing dabs of whipped cream to my nipples and a trail down my chest before tossing the bottle aside. She leans over me and rubs her tits on my chest, letting the cream cover her nipples as well, and I can't resist. My tongue darts out to lick it off, and she hums. We're both going to be a mess after this, and I'm already thinking of how I'm going to fuck her in the shower.

She licks the whipped cream off my nipple, then trails her tongue over to clean the other as well. My hands wander to her hair as she starts kissing a downward trail, and she sits up, shaking her head with a grin. "Hands back behind your head."

She's going to kill me.

I comply and watch her as she continues down to my cock. Fuck, but she's so good at this. It seems like she gets better every time. Part of it is the way she seems to love it. There's nothing like a blow job where the woman seems to be getting just as much out of it. Veronica teases and licks, tortures me with her lips and tongue, letting out the sexiest little hums and moans along the way.

I'm lost in the sensations, so close to coming, when I hear something that fills me with horror and panic.

"Veronica?"

Bailey's voice carries from the living room, getting closer as she adds. "Are you here? Dad's not home and I can't get in our apartment. I need our extra key."

"Fuck," I hiss, rolling off the bed as Veronica jumps off of me.

Panic controls my reaction, and I jerk on my underwear while Veronica hisses, "Window!"

Thank fuck we had it open, all I have to do is unlatch the bottom of the safety screen. It swings out, and I practically fall through it into the yard. It doesn't even occur to me that it's daylight, not even noon, and I'm now lying in the yard in my underwear, coated in whip cream and chocolate. It's running down my legs. I can feel it sticking my ass cheeks together as I leap to my feet.

There's nothing to do but make a mad dash for my apartment. I'm barely on my feet before I turn and run…right into Aiden's kiddie pool full of water. The plastic edge scratches both my shins, and I go down hard, face first in the tepid water, and I swear the splash couldn't have made more noise.

I scramble out of the pool, yanking my underwear up when the weight of the water makes them droop, and dart toward the street again. I just have to make it around the park without being seen.

No.

No, this isn't happening.

An ice cream truck sits right in front of the park, and I'm being stared at by no less than ten people—adults and kids—gathered around it. This is not the treat they were expecting. The sight freezes me in place for a moment, and I realize what they're seeing.

A man in nothing but soaking wet, white boxer briefs, with the crotch and ass stained brown. A mixture of chocolate and water runs down my legs, making it look to all the world like I just shit myself.

I can't blame them for gawping at me. Even for Violent Circle, this is pretty bad.

There's no explanation or apology that's going to cover this, and I still need to get home before Bailey sees me, so I just start running again. Raucous laughter follows me around the corner of my apartment. Of course, the Frat Hell guys would have to be out there.

My temporary relief at being out of view is crushed with the realization that my house keys are in my pants pocket on Veronica's floor. Fuck. I can't get in. And there's no way I can go back for my pants.

Leaning against the brick wall, I catch my breath and try to figure out what to do. How the hell did I get myself in this position? I'm not a damned teenager, but I sure feel like one at the moment.

Denton steps around the corner of the brick wall I'm ready

to bang my head against, and snorts out a laugh. "Dude, I lost the rock, paper, scissors challenge so I had to be the one to come see what the hell is going on."

With a groan, I lay my head back against the wall. "I didn't want Bailey to see me at Veronica's. She doesn't know we're seeing each other."

"And her finding out scared you so much that you shit yourself?"

"It's chocolate. Don't ask."

"Don't need to," he laughs, shaking his head. "Come on, we'll cut through the back yards to my place and you can clean up."

"Thanks." My head is on a swivel the whole walk to his apartment while I beg the universe to let me make it there without seeing anyone else.

The universe has a shitty sense of humor.

I make it to the apartment without running into any neighbors, but Denton failed to mention they had a damn cookout going on with half the kids from the college. As soon as we step inside, no less than eight pairs of eyes are on me, and the place falls silent.

The guys playing beer pong look up from the table, and someone pauses the video game the three people on the couch are playing.

Denton grins at my glare when I shake my head. "I hate you." The asshole wasn't trying to help. He was bringing the show home for his friends.

Jani and Noble take a second away from trying to devour each other's faces and both burst into laughter. "Having a bad day?" Jani asks.

"My ass cheeks are stuck together with chocolate. I've been better."

"Chocolate, sure, let's go with that," Noble says, and everyone laughs when I flip him off. "You can use my shower. There are shorts on my dresser you can borrow. You don't want Dent's pants, he has crabs." His gaze returns to my brown ass. "On second thought, keep the shorts."

"It's chocolate!" I insist, at the same time Denton yells, "I got rid of them months ago!"

I don't have time to delve into the subject of Denton's crotch critters. Bailey is home alone and wondering where I am. What the hell am I going to tell her?

Different stories run through my head as I shower, and I finally settle on something simple and hopefully believable.

Noble's shorts are made for his young, skinny, frame, but I manage to get them on. The moose knuckle I'm now sporting is in no way attractive. It looks like sad puppy dog eyes, and the walk home is only going to be slightly less embarrassing than my sprint home with the leaky ass look.

"Ow! Look at all that sexy!" Jani hoots when I return to the living room.

The laughter follows me through the apartment, and only fades when I've stepped out the back door. I manage to make it home without running into anyone else, and Bailey opens the back door when I tap on it.

"Uh…those aren't your shorts," she says as I step inside. Veronica stands behind her, trying not to laugh. Like she wasn't the one who doused me in chocolate and whipped cream in the first place.

"Yeah, I was at Noble's and one of the idiots spilled beer on me. Noble loaned me his shorts. Why are you back so quick? Did something happen?" Changing the subject seems the best way to go at this point.

"The spa was closed down by the health department because a bunch of people got a rash from their hot tub. Aunt Jill offered to take me with her to eat some vegan, farm to table, artisanal, locally sourced food, but I said no thanks."

Veronica pulls out a kitchen chair and has a seat. "You passed? You could've seen a man bun and handlebar mustache sporting hipster man in his natural habitat."

They delve into a conversation, and I slip out of the room to change clothes. At least Bailey bought my excuse. This time.

I'm too old for this shit.

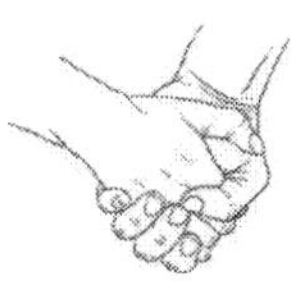

The phone call I got from George this morning put me in a great mood. He's found a place and we'll be able to move faster than I anticipated. It's a good time to get rid of some junk and get a head start on packing up.

Bailey looks up at me from the floor where she's sorting through DVD's as she packs them. "Can I give these kiddie cartoons to Aiden? I don't watch them anymore."

"Sure, just make a stack of whatever you don't want."

"I'm going to miss him and Veronica." It's the first negative thing she's said about the move. Up until now, she's been excited. Now that we're actually preparing to move, it's probably become real to her. This is the only place she can remember living, so of course she'll miss her childhood home, especially because it wasn't such a bad place until the new management took over.

"You'll still see them often. They'll still be our friends."

Bailey chews her lip and nods. "Becky has a boyfriend now. And since they got together, she hardly talks to me or any of her other friends. They just spend all their time together."

It's funny but horrifying how serious kids seem to be about middle school relationships. I'm not sure why she's comparing moving away from our friends though, until she continues, "Amber said it was the same way with her older sister. Once they're dating, they don't have time for anyone else."

"That's not how a healthy relationship works, but you guys are a little young to worry about that stuff right now."

"I know, but if Veronica starts dating that firefighter she likes, she might forget about us when we aren't right across the street."

I freeze, my hand halfway to the box I'm packing. "What firefighter?"

Bailey shrugs, popping open a DVD case to check that the disc is inside before adding it to the box. "She met him when he came to the hotel, the day the sprinklers destroyed everything."

Clueless she's just blown my world apart, she gets to her feet and heads out the door. "I'm going to take these DVD's to Aiden."

The sprinkler catastrophe was a long time ago, and she never mentioned him to me. I know we haven't made promises to each other or anything, but the time we spent together at the hotel...I thought we were on the same page. It's been on the tip of my tongue to start a conversation with Bailey about how she'd feel if I was in a relationship. I was just waiting for the right time.

Fuck, maybe I waited too long.

Anger and jealousy war inside me as I picture Veronica with some asshole tough guy who gets women by running into burning buildings. Fuck. No.

Not fucking happening.

Chapter Twelve

Veronica

Bailey sits at my table, eating a popsicle while Aiden looks through the DVD's she's just brought him.

"Mom!" he pipes up. "Can I watch Batman?"

"Don't turn the TV up too loud," I warn, and he rushes off. By the look on Bailey's face, she's got something on her mind.

"Bailey, is something wrong?"

"We're starting to get packed. We'll be moving soon."

I'd give up a kidney to move into a nice house like the one she's getting, but I understand her apprehension. She's grown up here. "I know moving is hard, but you'll still be close by. You can come over and hang out, play with the friends you have here."

Her next words wound something growing inside of me that I hadn't even let myself admit was there. "Will you and Dad still be friends if he starts dating the lady from the dollar store?"

"What lady?" Pausing, I take a deep breath. I didn't mean to snap at her, but the words just sort of flew out.

Nonplussed, she shrugs. "Some lady that Dad met at the dollar store. They talk all night on the phone. He doesn't think I know."

You have no right to be jealous, I tell myself. Over and over, I let that reminder beat through my head. No right to be jealous. No right.

It doesn't change the fact that an ache has settled in my chest, right on top of the emptiness in my middle. Swallowing hard, I think carefully before answering her. "It doesn't matter who your Dad dates, you and I will always be friends and you'll always be able to come and visit anytime."

The corner of her lip tucks in. "It won't be the same."

I try to swallow down the sudden panic and heartache that has gripped me and sit across from her.

"Not exactly the same, I know. But that's life, honey. The next few years are going to be full of changes for you. You'll go to middle school, then high school, meet new friends, and experience new things. It'll be scary, but a whole lot of fun too. And you can always come and talk to me."

Nodding, she gets to her feet. "Thanks. I'd better get back. We're cleaning out closets. We might have a yard sale."

"Let me know if you need anything."

I feel a little bad as she leaves because I know she's upset, but it was everything I could do not to burst into tears. Which is stupid. Neal and I decided from the beginning that we were just screwing around, that we wouldn't get serious because it wouldn't be good for the kids.

It just felt like more. Watching him teach Aiden to ride his bike, helping me by cutting the grass at Mom's, spending hours at night cuddled together in bed, talking about anything and everything until the sky started to lighten.

Spending all that time at the hotel wasn't a good idea. It felt too much like a relationship and made me lose the grip on what we are; two single parents helping each other out with the kids. And an occasional orgasm. So why does it feel like someone scooped out my insides and filled me with sand? That's the best way I can describe the disappointment and sudden regret weighing me down. Heavy.

I need to talk to someone because this is crazy. Neal isn't my boyfriend.

I grab my phone and text Emily.

Me: What are you doing tonight?

Emily: No plans. I'm off tomorrow.
Me: Me too. Want to get drunk?
Emily: Name the time and place.
Me: Let me get back to you. See if I can find a sitter.

I'm sure as hell not asking Neal. I don't want to see him right now because there's no way I can act like everything is okay. He has no idea I know about this other woman. Instead, I text Noble.

Me: Hey, I'm looking for a sitter tonight. Would you or Denton want to make $25 to stay with Aiden?

It doesn't take him long to reply.

Noble: Do you mind if Jani joins me?
Me: Not at all. Seven?
Noble: I'll be there.

Emily and I make plans to meet at my place and taxi to a bar in the next little town. I'm not looking to meet anyone else. I just want to drown my sorrows and talk to a friend who might be able to help me work out what the hell I'm feeling, but I'm still dressing to kill tonight. I need to feel beautiful. Getting passed over for the dollar store lady is hell on a girl's self-esteem.

"Ade, I'm going to go see Emily tonight. Noble and Jani are coming to watch you. I want you to be good and go to bed when they tell you to."

"Can we play video games?" He looks up from the table where he's scarfing down a hot dog and mac and cheese.

"Yeah, after you finish eating, you can play."

"Yes!"

A little over an hour later, Emily shows up and whistles. "You look great. Can't remember the last time I saw you in a dress."

Maybe because I don't own a lot of dresses. I'm much more a jeans and t-shirt kind of person, but my form fitting little black dress makes my slight curves look more pronounced. My hair—that's more often tied up in a ponytail than not—hangs around my face, straight, and sleek. A light layer of makeup hides my pale skin's flaws and makes my eyes pop. I don't look like me, but I think I like it. Tonight, I want to be someone else.

Noble and Jani show up right after, and Aiden instantly drags Noble over to the video games.

"Damn," Jani says, grinning at me. "You out to get laid tonight?"

"Nope, just trying to blow off some steam."

"Well, if it turns into an all nighter, just text me. I don't mind staying."

Noble gives me a strange look before asking, "Where's Neal tonight?"

"Home, I assume." A honk from outside saves the day. "Our taxi is here. You both have my number." I give Aiden a quick kiss goodnight that he swats away, focused on his game.

"Thanks guys!" I call out to Noble and Jani as we're leaving.

Emily turns to me once we're in the taxi. "So, do you want to tell me what happened? Because I've never known you to want to hit the bar last minute."

"I need a drink first."

"Okay."

One thing I always dread is that first moment you walk into a bar. Everyone turns to look at you and this time is no different. My forced smile probably doesn't hide my sudden nerves as I try not to trip or do anything stupid. By the time we choose a table, everyone's attention has wandered away again. Whew.

The place is packed, and we were lucky to get a table, even though it's next to a table full of loud guys who are probably from the college, by the looks of them. We order drinks from the waitress, and Emily waits until we're sipping our fruity alcohol to ask again. "So, what happened?"

"I'm an idiot," I sigh. "I thought I could just fuck Neal with no strings attached and keep emotions out of it. But today, I found out he's seeing someone else and…it hurts. I don't have the right to be jealous. But I want to find the dollar store bitch and scratch her eyes out."

Emily sits up and signals the waitress. "Two more Margaritas. And two shots of Jaeger."

She shoves my drink toward me. "Drink that, because we're going to get fucked up, then you're going to listen to me, because I have a lot to say."

A giggle escapes me despite my somber mood. I love how blunt she is. I knew she was the person to go to if I wanted to put things in perspective. We down our drinks, then the shots, and begin sipping our second margaritas. Warmth spreads from my stomach out, and I feel my muscles relax a bit.

"Okay," Emily begins. "First, how do you know he's seeing someone?"

"Bailey told me. She was worried because they're moving soon. She doesn't know we were more than friends—she's only eleven—but she was worried a girlfriend in the mix would keep us all from hanging out."

"Smart kid," Emily murmurs. "You don't know how long they've been seeing each other?"

"No, all I know is she said they talk all night on the phone."

Emily sips her drink. "Then he may not be sleeping with her."

"It doesn't matter. We aren't together. I shouldn't care."

"Veronica, just because you two said you wouldn't be serious doesn't mean you weren't. You spent every moment together. For months. You take care of each other's children. You go places together, eat meals together, hang out constantly at your place or his. Like it or not, even without the sex, that's a relationship. You two can deny it until the end of always, but it's still true.

"I understand you didn't make any promises to each other, but that doesn't mean he shouldn't let you know he's dating someone and give you the option to stop what you're doing. Let me ask you something. What if it were the other way around? If you had met someone and accepted a date with him, would you have told Neal? Or would you hide it and go on fucking him?"

Damn, she's making sense.

"It's different. I wouldn't accept the date in the beginning. I told you that firefighter asked me out when I ran into him again." Shaking my head, I drain my glass. "I never even considered it. I was in a hurry to get back to Neal. We were taking the kids to the lake."

Her gaze meets mine. "You want my honest opinion?"

"Of course."

"You've nailed the issue right there. If he's willing to date and hide it from you, then I don't think he feels the same way you do. Or he's just an asshole. Either way, it leads to the same."

Sighing, I sit back in my chair, trying to accept what is clear. "It's over. Whatever it was."

Emily's expression softens. "I'm not saying he doesn't care about you. Any idiot can see that he does. I think there are some men who just don't settle down, and if he's still playing games at his age, maybe he's one of them."

I signal the waitress for another drink. "We never should've slept together. I don't want to lose him completely, especially because Aiden adores him, but I think I need some distance for a while." Emily smiles when I ask, "Any advice on how to get over someone I never should've been under?"

"Get under someone new?"

Laughing, I shake my head. "Not my style." My gaze is drawn to the dance floor where a throng of gyrating bodies clash and move together. There are quite a few young guys here tonight. "But I wouldn't mind rubbing my drunk ass all over one of these guys on the dance floor."

"Ha!" Emily gets to her feet. "Are you drunk? Good. Let's go have some fun."

The next few hours are a blur of alcohol, laughter, and sweaty male bodies pressed to mine. I don't remember any of the guy's names, but it doesn't matter. I'm not going home with anyone, just having fun and reminding myself that Neal isn't the only man in the world. Even if he's the only man in my world. What did I just tell Bailey?

Life is change.

And getting trashed and dancing with strangers is a definite change for me.

Emily stumbles back to the table, a man's arm wrapped around her. Where do I recognize him from? Oh, it's the guy who comes in the laundromat with a bunch of kid's clothes every week. The same one she's been drooling over from a distance. She's been dancing with him all night, so I'm surprised I didn't notice before.

"Veronica, this is Lincoln."

"Nice to meet you."

"Good to meet you too," he says. He excuses himself to go to the bar, and Emily plops down across from me with a squeal.

"I finally talked to him! Oh, Veronica, he's so great. I know he's older, but I don't give half a fuck."

"You were worried about him having a bunch of kids," I remind her. I'm not trying to douse her happiness. I'm glad to see she finally made a move, but she's drunk so a reminder seems prudent.

"He doesn't! All that laundry he brings in is from his neighbor's kids. They're poor and she's a single mom so he helps her out. Isn't that sooo sweet?" She sighs and lays her head on her arm, her cheeks pink with alcohol.

"It really is," I agree.

"I'm going to fuck him. Tonight. God, it's been so long."

Laughing at how quickly that escalated, I ask, "Is he aware of this?"

"He offered to drive us home since he's only had two beers. I told him I might need help making it to my bed," she laughs.

"Subtle."

"Right?"

Lincoln returns with two bottles of water, hands them to us and takes a seat. While they make goo goo eyes at each other, the next table of college guys becomes another source of entertainment.

They're drunk and talking louder than they think they are about who is the worst at getting women.

A slurring blond, maybe about twenty-two years old,

states, "You guys just have to learn to be smooth like me."

His friend snorts. "Uh-huh, like when you tried to get Molly to go home with you?"

"Hey, her loss, doesn't mean my game was faulty."

"You winked and pointed finger guns at her."

His table cracks up laughing, and Emily and I join in, but they don't seem to notice.

"That's not as bad as when he tried to get my neighbor to go out with him," another guy speaks up.

"What?" The blond glares at him, looking offended. "I said she was pretty!"

"You told her she was quite comely, and she laughed at you. I was waiting for you to suggest courting her."

"Fuck off, at least I fucked Samantha."

His friend scoffs. "Like that's so hard to do. She's got that whore jaw. It dislocates when it sees dick."

He grins. "Yeah, her tits kind of turned me off too. She had nipples the size of a McGriddle. And she smelled like hot dog water."

That does it. Emily and I both fall into hysterics. Lincoln chuckles and shakes his head at us. Emily's gaze meets mine, and I know she's wondering the same thing as me. Is it our neighbor Samantha?

"Are you two ready to go?" Lincoln asks.

"Yeah, I think I've sweated off all my makeup," I laugh.

Lincoln seems amused by our drunken conversation on the ride home, though he doesn't say anything.

"Fuck Neal and his dollar store whore," I say, laughing. The world outside the car slides by in a smear of colors and lights. "God, why don't I do this more often? I feel great. We should do this every week."

I roll the window down and lay my head on the sill, letting the wind blow through my damp hair.

"We should!" Emily agrees.

Lincoln chuckles and grins at her. "I think you two will have a different opinion tomorrow."

"Psh, that's future Veronica's problem. Present Veronica is

happy as fuck."

Emily laughs when her stomach growls. "Present Emily is starving."

"Tacos!" I exclaim, probably a little too loudly. "We need tacos."

Turning into the fast food restaurant just down the street from us, Lincoln says, "You'll definitely be hating life tomorrow."

A few minutes later, we pull up in front of my apartment. "Just park here," Emily directs. "I'm only a couple doors down and there's never a spot."

Laughing, we all pile out of the car. Somehow, the humid air reaches out and trips me. I stumble into Lincoln, trying to hang onto my food and not eat a mouthful of grass. He grabs me and holds my arm a moment, steadying me.

"Thanks. Sorry I stepped on your foot."

"No problem."

Emily opens her mouth to say something, but she doesn't get a chance. Neal marches out my front door, glaring at Lincoln's hand on my arm. "What the fuck are you doing?" Before anyone can say anything, he snaps at Lincoln. "Who the fuck are you?"

Whoa.

Stop the train.

My drunken brain takes a second to catch up, but once it does, rage blooms in the pit of my stomach.

Controlling my temper, temporarily, I nod at Lincoln. "Thanks for getting us home safely."

He glances up at a simmering Neal, then focuses on me. "Are you okay here?"

"Yep. All good."

"She's fine," Emily agrees, winking at me and pulling Lincoln toward her apartment. "And she has my number if she needs me."

They walk away, and I turn to face Neal, a hundred different emotions roiling inside me. "Just what the hell was that?"

His frown deepens. "Where were you? Have you been drinking?"

"Not since I left the bar."

He scowls and crosses his arms. "You don't drink."

Somebody help me because I'm fighting the urge to kick him in the shins like a toddler throwing a tantrum. All the hurt I've felt today after finding out about his other woman mixes with anger, and all I want to do is make him feel the way I do.

"I don't dance all night with hot college guys either, but maybe I should more often. Tonight was just what I needed. And it's none of your damned business what I do!"

He grabs my arm as I start toward the house, and I lose my temper. He's seeing someone else while he's fucking me, and he has the nerve to get pissed I went out without telling him?

"I'm not a child, Neal. And you can't tell me what to do. You can fuck right off!" Great, I've joined the Violent Circle tradition of screaming and fighting in the yard. I'm so pissed that he's got me worked up to this point and ruined a fun night when I was already struggling. I don't kick him in the shins, but my reaction isn't much better. Jerking away from him, I throw the greasy bag in my hand right at his head, and it explodes in a burst of meat, lettuce and cheese, raining down on his head and the ground.

Noble and Jani step out onto my porch, and Neal tears his glare from me, realizing we have an audience. "I'll talk to you tomorrow when you're sober," he says.

But he'll probably go home and call the dollar store bitch tonight. "Don't bother. I don't need anything from the dollar store. Least of all some kind of crotch rot." I throw my final words back as I march toward the house.

If he responds, I don't hear it. My heart is beating in my ears, and all I want to do is get inside.

Jani follows me in and sits down while I head for the bathroom to relieve my screaming bladder.

A glance in the mirror shows me what a mess I am, and I stand there for a moment, trying to find my equilibrium. Nothing shows you how drunk you are like being alone in a bathroom. It's always then I seem to notice. Once I've relieved myself and pulled my emotions under control, I return to the living room and flop onto the couch.

"I'm so shitfaced." Silence reigns for a moment until Jani's gaze meets mine and we both break into laughter. "Did I scare Noble off?"

"I think he went over to Neal's."

After a few seconds, I kick my shoes off. "I threw my taco at him."

Jani snorts out a laugh. "Not the one you wanted to throw at him."

My hands rise to cover my hot face. "We just confirmed the rumor for the whole neighborhood. Funny, since it won't be true anymore. We're done. Not that we were ever really together." Leaning over, I lay my head on the arm of the couch. Damn, this is comfortable. Why did I never realize how comfortable my couch was? "Aiden go to bed okay?"

"Yeah, he's out like a light. Don't worry."

"Thanks."

My eyes fall closed for a second until I hear Aiden's voice. "Mom? Why did you sleep on the couch? Did you know Jani is in your bed? Where is Noble? Can I go play with Bailey?"

What fresh hell am I in now? My eyelids feel like they're glued shut, and it takes a second for me to force them open. I'm sorry the second I do, and they slam shut against the bright sunlight.

Shit. I passed out on the couch. And now, I feel like warmed over garbage. "Give me a minute to wake up, Ade," I grumble. As soon as I sit up, my head spins, and I dart for the bathroom.

Dry heaves suck. One of the basic rules of drinking is to eat before and after. Fucking Neal. I wouldn't be sick if the tacos had made it into my stomach instead of the yard. Oh god. Last night I made a complete idiot of myself screaming in the front yard. I'm never drinking again.

"Mom?" Aiden pops open the door to see me sitting on the floor. "Are you sick?"

"Just a little. Go get yourself some cereal and watch cartoons for a bit, okay?"

"Okay."

Jani enters a moment later with a bottle of water and a wet

washcloth. "Thanks. And thanks for staying. I didn't mean to get that messed up."

Jani grins at me. "No worries. Looked like you needed it."

"The whole neighborhood is going to be talking about me," I groan.

"Only until something else happens. And Darla just put a creepy mannequin in her front window. She hangs that floppy sunhat on it when she isn't wearing it."

Aiden pokes his head in the room. "She isn't a witch, Mom! Eddie told me she's a witch, but he's wrong."

"There's no such thing as witches, Ade." God his voice is piercing my brain.

"I know! She's a vampire! That's why she covers up when she comes out in the daylight."

Aiden has me fighting back a laugh, despite how miserable I feel. "She's not a vampire. And you'd better not be rude to her."

"She is! I swear! She told everyone she's from Pennsylvania, and that's where vampires are from!"

It takes my slow, alcohol pickled brain a moment to catch up, but Jani cracks up first.

"Transylvania," she laughs, holding her stomach. "It's Transylvania, Aiden. Not Pennsylvania."

Aiden chews on that for a moment and then shrugs. "Oh, okay." He looks behind him as there's a tap on the door. "I ate my cereal. Can I go to the park with Eddie and Bailey?"

"Yes, but you come home if Bailey goes home."

"I will!" he shouts, running out the door.

"I love that kid," Jani says, still chuckling. "Get a shower and I'll go grab us a nice greasy breakfast from the diner."

"Thank you," I breathe, pulling some money from my pocket. "Grab Noble something too. I owe you both for last night."

As soon as she leaves, I drag my ass into the shower. At least the thumping of my head is distracting me from my thoughts of Neal. There are parts of last night that are a little fuzzy, but I remember him acting like a total asshole for no reason. I'm the one who should've been mad.

Sadness washes over me when I realize I feel a little

relieved he'll be moving soon. It's going to be hard enough to get over him without watching whoever he dates go in and out of his apartment.

I hate this.

We never should've stepped over that friend line.

I pop a couple painkillers after my shower and walk outside to check that Aiden is at the park with Bailey. Aiden and Eddie play on the swings, but Bailey runs over to the fence. "Veronica! Dad is going to take me and Aiden to get ice cream! Want to go?"

"No thanks, honey. I don't feel too great today." I dig in my pocket and hand her a five-dollar bill. "Give this to your dad for Aiden."

She bites her lip and stares at me for a second before taking the bill.

"Have fun," I tell her, plastering a smile on my face. She watches as I return to the apartment to meet Jani and Noble.

Aiden flies through the door a few minutes later and thrusts the money at me. "Neal said don't assault him! We're going to The Cold Hut!" With that, he's right back out the door.

Jani and Noble both look up at me as I say, "Assault him?"

Noble grins and shovels food into his mouth. "Insult him, probably."

He barely gets the words out when I get a text from Neal.

Neal: We need to talk.

Aren't those the worst fucking words? It's never good, and I just don't see the point. He's dating, and I'm jealous. I need time, not words.

Me: I need some space. Please don't contact me unless it's about the kids. And please make sure Bailey understands she's always welcome here.

He doesn't respond. I don't hear from him at all until he texts a few days later to let me know there's a movie night taking place for the kids at the community center.

I've tried my best not to let Aiden see how devastated I've been since that day. I don't think he's noticed much of a change since he still gets to hang out at Neal's and Bailey still comes here. That five-year-old self-absorption has been a godsend.

Chapter Thirteen

Neal

The community center looks closed when I go to pick up Bailey. The only cars in the lot belong to Noble and Veronica. It's strange considering there are usually a lot of kids anytime the center offers an activity.

The place is as quiet as a graveyard, and my footsteps echo down the long, dim hallway as I make my way down to the gym. "Bailey?"

Jani pops her head out of the gym door and beckons me before retreating back inside. What the hell?

When I step into the gym, Jani and Bailey stand there, Jani with a wide grin, and Bailey gnawing her lip. "Bails? What's going on?"

"I-I need to tell you something," she mumbles.

Jani pats her on the shoulder and says, "I'll be right out in the hall."

Fear filters in as I wonder what she could be so fearful of telling me. If her mother has been contacting her without my knowledge...

"I'm so sorry," Bailey says, and her tears well over. "I screwed everything up."

"Bailey, whatever it is, it'll be okay." We take a few steps until we can take a seat on the stairs leading to the stage. "Just tell me. Are you in some kind of trouble?"

She shakes her head and wipes her eyes. "It's my fault you and Veronica aren't friends anymore."

Damn it all. This type of thing was exactly what we were trying to keep from happening. "No, honey, it's not. And we are friends. We just..."

"Can't stand to be around each other," she scoffs, giving me a look filled with wisdom beyond her age. "But it's my fault." She takes a deep breath. "I lied."

"You lied about what?"

"I lied when I said Veronica was seeing a firefighter. I overheard her talking to Emily. She was telling her a firefighter asked her out, but that she said no. And Emily asked her why. She said it was because of you. Because she could only think about you, but that you didn't want to be together."

She wasn't seeing anyone else. All the anger and jealousy I've been trying to tamp down was for nothing. Relief fills me, but I know it may not matter now. It suddenly clicks into place what that weird comment Veronica made about crotch rot from a dollar store might have been about. I just chalked it up to drunk talk. When she said she needed space, I assumed she'd decided to give it a go with the firefighter.

My instinct was to put a stop to it. To inform her she's mine and drag her back to my place like a Neanderthal. My reaction when she returned from the bar that night scared the shit out of me because I don't lose control like that. It's not who I am. I left her alone for both our sakes, because I've been teetering on the edge of crazy at the thought of her with anyone else.

"Did you tell Veronica I was seeing someone?"

Looking at the floor, Bailey nods. "I told her there was a lady you talked on the phone to all night. I thought if you both got jealous, you'd change your mind and get married. She could be my mom and Aiden could be my little brother."

Bailey is usually so mature for her age, that there are times I forget she's not even twelve years old. It takes something like this to let me see how naive and innocent she really is. What has really caught me off guard is her wish for a mother. She's never said anything, and I've avoided relationships to spare her feelings.

"Bailey, do you remember when I took my wedding ring off?"

"Yes."

"You remember how upset you were?"

She looks up at me. "That was years ago. I just wanted Mom to come home. When you took off the ring, I knew it wasn't going to happen. I was nine. I didn't understand."

She leans against me when I put my arm around her. "I know that, honey. I'm not scolding you over it. It was understandable. But I don't want to do anything to hurt you. You're the most important girl in my life, no matter what. You know that, don't you?"

She hugs me. "I know, but I don't want to be the only one. I want you to be happy too. And I love Veronica."

Sighing, I squeeze her back. "So do I, Bails, but love doesn't always lead to marriage. Even if I started seeing Veronica again, or another woman in the future, it doesn't mean we'll get married."

"I know."

I look down at her, making sure she's looking me in the eye. "You can't manipulate people, Bailey. Especially not by using their feelings against them. It's wrong, and you aren't going to get the outcome you want."

Nodding, tears streak down her face again. "I know that now. I'm sorry."

"I know. Some lessons we have to learn the hard way, kid, but those are the ones that stick with us."

Bailey sits up and fidgets with her hands. "So, um...would having Noble and Jani set up a romantic dinner for you and Veronica in the lunchroom, then getting you both to show up be considered manipulating? Because if so, I swear, this is the last time."

"Wait, what?"

Noble steps in, dressed in a tuxedo with a towel draped over his arm like a waiter in a fancy restaurant. "Your lady awaits, sir," he announces, biting back a laugh.

Bailey looks up at me with a combination of hope and caution. "She's waiting for you. Well, sort of. She's waiting for something. Aiden just told her she had a surprise."

Surreal isn't a sufficient word as I follow Noble down the hall and peek into the lunchroom that has been decked out like a restaurant. White tablecloths, candles, the whole shebang.

At the center table, Veronica sits, looking casually beautiful as she glances around like something might explode. "You'd better go in before she leaves. She's not very patient," Noble says. "I'll be bringing your food."

"Did you set this up?"

"Dude, I don't have a vagina. Bailey came to me, and I owed her one after she helped me get Jani back. The whole neighborhood knows you two should be together, so I got Jani to help. Now get in there and don't fuck this up. Jani and I are taking Aiden and Bailey back to Jani's apartment tonight. We'll send them home in the morning."

This is crazy. Completely and totally insane. But there's not an inch of me that doesn't want her, so I step into the lunchroom slash impromptu fancy restaurant.

"Neal?" Her jaw tenses and the little *I'm pissed* lines pop up around her mouth. "What's going on? Did you do this?"

Sighing, I sit across from her. "Nope, we've been parent trapped."

"What the hell are you talking about?"

"Bailey got Noble and Jani to lure us together."

She rubs her forehead. "Shit. Is Bailey upset?"

Noble appears, still carrying the towel over his arm and walking stiffly. Is that how he thinks waiters walk? He shuffles over to fill our wine glasses and starts speaking in a horrible accent. It's like a mix of Italian and French and probably borderline offensive to both nationalities.

"Ciao, welcome to Little Italy. It's-uh me, Noble. We are appy to ave you and your usband. We will start with the wine and then-uh the pasta, no?"

"Dude, stop, you sound like Mario. Give us a minute, okay?"

"Very well. I-uh know when I'm a not-uh wanted." He

keeps mumbling in the horrible accent as he leaves, but I'm focused on Veronica.

"Bailey is okay. V, I want to apologize for the way I acted. Bailey told me you were dating a firefighter and—"

"I'm not dating anyone!" she interrupts. "Why would she say that?"

"For the same reason she told you I was talking to some woman on the phone all night. She wanted to make us jealous because she thought it would push us together."

Veronica sits back, her mouth slightly open as the realization sinks in. "There was no dollar store whore?"

"No. And you haven't been seeing anyone?"

"No."

She picks up her wine and takes a few gulps. We stare at one another for a few seconds until a smile cracks her lips, followed by a giggle. It is funny in a way, and my laughter fills the room along with hers.

"She set us up, and it backfired," she clarifies.

"Then she had Noble and Jani help her try to fix it. By doing this." I gesture around the room.

"And they agreed. They all think if you just put us in the same room..."

"Like two pandas," I snort. "Just lock us together and we'll be all over each other."

When our laughter dies down, I reach across and lay my hand on hers. "I've missed you. I'm sorry. It doesn't matter what I thought or what I was told. I should've talked to you. I was an asshole."

She squeezes my hand. "You tried to talk to me. I'm sorry too. I knew I had no right to be angry that you were talking to someone else, but it tore me up. It made me realize we've been fooling ourselves, thinking we could just be friends."

She sighs and pulls her hand back. "I know it's hard on us, but we need to make sure the kids aren't suffering because we made a mistake. Bailey can always come to see me. I've come to love her like my own."

She still thinks this isn't going to happen.

"Do you love me?"

Tears fill her eyes and she nods. "I'm sorry."

"You're sorry for loving me?"

She nods. "I know that wasn't supposed to happen."

"V, I love you too, and damn what we thought was supposed to happen. This." I point back and forth between us. "Us. We happened. And I don't regret a second of it. I'm also not ready for it to end."

"But...we said...the kids..."

"I love Aiden. He's the son I didn't have."

"He loves you too, but—"

"But what? They might suffer if we broke up? They'd be right where we are now. We can't be afraid of the *if's* anymore. What *if* things work out and we make a family? What *if* we get to spend the rest of our lives with the people we love? A clean start for both of us."

Swallowing hard, she grins through her tears. "Are you asking me to be your girlfriend, Neal?"

"No, I'm asking you to move in with me and be my everything. And one day soon, when I'm sure you won't run away screaming, I'll be asking for you to be my wife. Because that's how this story ends, V. With you and me."

She gets to her feet, and I meet her halfway around the table.

My arms wrap around her as she adds, "And hours of dirty, sweaty fucking."

Our mouths clash together in a kiss that displays the desperation we've both felt. Her hands grip my hair and she throws her legs around my waist as I back her against the wall, losing myself in her the way I've dreamed of every night she's been gone.

Everything around us disappears. I don't care that she's ten years younger, that we'll have to make adjustments for the kids, or that we're in the middle of a lunchroom in a damn community center. All I can see and feel is her.

Until Noble's voice echoes around us.

"You couldn't even wait until after the spaghetti?" He

grumbles and puts two plates on the table before heading toward the door mumbling, "Like freaking rabbits."

Veronica laughs and calls out, "More like pandas, actually."

Chapter Fourteen

Veronica

The next few weeks are busy, but fantastic. We have a talk with the kids, and they're thrilled we'll be moving in together. My lease isn't up for a few months, so I have more time than Neal to get packed up, but there's some work we'd like to do with the place anyway, and it helps that we can crash at my apartment when the water is shut off or the smell of paint is overpowering.

We both have the day off work today, and we're shopping for household stuff. Aiden is at daycare, and Bailey is spending the day with a friend. It's nice to be able to take our time and not have to drag the kids around with us.

Neal wraps his arm around me as we make our way through the parking lot and into the store. We've been so touchy feely it probably makes our friends gag, but I don't care. It feels amazing to be able to touch him and not worry about the kids seeing.

We fill the cart with curtain rods, window treatments, and various other necessities. While I'm trying to decide on a shower curtain for the bathroom, Neal plants a soft kiss on my temple. "I'm going to go next door to get some paint. Meet you in the car?"

I smile up at him. He's been patient as I've meandered around the store, trying to find the perfect things to make the new house a home. I'm sure he's dying to escape. "Sure, I'll just be a few more minutes."

His chuckle tells me he knows as well as I do that's bullshit. But really, we have to look at this shower curtain every day. It needs to be perfect.

Finally, I settle on a pretty yellow one and head to the cashier. As I'm checking out, I see the last person I want to see, loitering outside the plate glass window. He has his back to me, but I'd know that haircut and jacket from anywhere. Clint. And I have to walk past him.

Forcing my chin high and prepared to fight, I make my way out of the store with my bags in hand. My heart leaps into my throat when I look at him and see something new. His left leg below the knee has been replaced with a blue metal prosthetic. It hasn't been that long since I saw him, so what the hell happened?

The words jump out before I can think about them as I approach him. "Oh my god, what happened to your leg?"

My gaze is fixated on his prosthetic until I hear a very unfamiliar voice reply, "I lost it to cancer a few years ago, but I don't see how it's any of your business."

My eyes climb slowly to his face, and I want to die.

Or at least be dragged away, maybe into that nearby sewer grate, where no one can see me. Where is that killer clown when you need him?

It's not Clint.

The angry eyes that pierce me are brown, not blue. "Oh god. I'm so sorry. I thought you were someone else. Someone I knew. My ex, who ran out on his kid. I'm so so sorry."

My rambling response brings a slight smile to the man's face, but I don't stick around to see what he says. My face is burning up, and I just want to get away. I rush into the parking lot, squinting against the sun glinting off the cars, and frantically try to remember where Neal parked. Oh, I hope he didn't see that.

Finally, I spot his car and damn it, I can make out a figure in the driver's seat. At least he couldn't have heard what I asked the guy. Eyes on the pavement, I rush over, throw the back door open and toss in the bags. I jump into the front seat, lay my hand on his knee, and exclaim, “Please get me out of here. I made a total idiot of myself just now.”

Silence descends as I squeeze my eyes shut, waiting to feel the car move me away from the source of my embarrassment. “Uh…Ma’am?”

What the?

My eyes pop open at yet another unfamiliar voice, and I’m afraid to turn my head. Because if what I suspect is true, I will never be able to forget this day. Finally, I look over at the man in the driver’s seat. The man who looks nothing like Neal because he isn’t Neal because I’m in the wrong damn car.

I don’t know what’s worse. Realizing I still have my hand on his knee, hearing this man chuckle, or looking over to the next car that happens to be the same model and color, where Neal sits, laughing his damn ass off.

This should be the moment I wake up because there’s no way I can accept what has happened in the last five minutes. “Sorry,” I mumble. “Wrong car.” I’m out in a flash and I fling myself into Neal’s car, wishing it was a bottomless abyss.

Pulling my knees up, I drop my head and cover my face. “I can’t believe I did that.”

Neal’s laugh echoes around me. “I should be insulted you don’t know what I look like.”

“The sun was in my eyes and…please, just get me out of here,” I moan, not uncovering my face.

There’s a tap on Neal’s window, and I peek up long enough to see the man standing there with a smile, waving my bags I left in his back seat. This really can’t get any worse.

Neal takes the bags and thanks the man. Finally, I feel the car move, but I don’t look up until we’re parked at my apartment again.

Neal’s hand creeps onto my leg. “V?”

“Hmm?”

“You going to go turtle for the rest of the day?” Amusement rings in his voice.

“The rest of the year sounds better.”

Chuckling, he squeezes my knee. “Come on, so you got in

the wrong car. I was the only one who saw it."

"Yeah," I scoff. "Only the person whose opinion means the most to me." As usual, I don't give the words much thought before they leap past my lips.

When I look up, a grin is inching across his face. The corners of his eyes wrinkle a tiny bit as the grin turns to a full, incredulous smile. "My opinion means the most to you?"

"What? No." My reply is light and teasing. "Of course not. Why would I care what an old man like you thinks of me?"

His hands land on my cheeks as he plants his lips on mine for a long, sensuous kiss. When we break apart, he says, "Secret's out, V. You love me. Worship the ground I walk on. It's understandable. I'm awesome."

Giggling, I shake my head. "Can we just get out of the car and pretend the last hour never happened?"

"We can get out of the car. Can't promise the rest."

Once we unload our purchases, we take a seat in my living room. He sits back on the couch, and reaches to play with the ends of my hair. "We need to find a babysitter for this weekend."

"We do?"

"Mmm Hmm. I'm taking you on a date. We've never been anywhere without the kids."

He's right. It hadn't even occurred to me. I cuddle against him "Well, we never do anything the typical way, do we?"

"What fun would that be?"

Neal doesn't mention the date again until he tells me that Noble agreed to stay at my apartment to watch the kids. "Are you okay with leaving Aiden with him for twenty-four hours?"

"Yeah, Aiden loves Noble. He'll have a blast." I peek up at him. "Where are we going?"

"You'll see."

"Tease. I need to know what to wear."

He slips his hand under my hair, running his fingers across the back of my neck. It always drives me crazy and he knows it. "Comfortable clothes. No dresses as much as I'd love to peel you out of one. You'll want to bring a swimsuit."

The suspense is killing me, and he grins at my impatience

when I try to get him to say more. "Just go pack a bag. Noble will be here in an hour. I'll go tell the kids."

An hour later, we're on our way, and I have no idea where we're going as we pull onto the highway. "How long is the drive?"

"A couple of hours."

I pester him on and off throughout the next two hours, but he won't tell me anything until he turns off the highway and onto a winding country road and I exclaim, "A lake? Did you rent us a cabin or something?"

"Better," he replies with a grin. "A cabin cruiser."

Excited, I sit up and crane my neck to see the lake behind the tree line as it blurs past. "We're going on a boat? I've never been on a boat."

He parks at a Marina and stares at me. "Really? Not even a pedal boat, canoe, nothing?"

"No, Mom can't swim so we didn't do much water stuff when I was young."

His face glows with happiness at getting to show me something new. "You're going to love spending the night on the lake."

Spending the night? Out on a pitch dark lake? The idea suddenly sounds as terrifying as exhilarating, but there's no way I'll let him see my nervousness. "We're going to sleep on a boat?" What kind of boat is a cabin cruiser? And what if I need the bathroom? A thousand questions run through my head as we make our way inside and Neal makes arrangements with the man renting us the boat.

When we're lead out to the Cabin Cruiser, my eyes widen in appreciation. It's not the tiny boat I was expecting. I could easily spend a weekend on it and be comfortable. The deck is large, with plenty of seating and easy access in and out of the water. A few steps lead down to a small kitchen, bathroom, and bed.

"This is amazing," I squeal! "I could live here."

Neal laughs at my enthusiasm, and we unload the trunk of his car. He's thought of everything. A cooler of food and drinks, sunblock, towels, anything we might need for the next twenty-four hours.

"We should charge our phones first," I caution. "In case the kids call tonight."

"There's a generator. We'll have electricity."

A firm breeze whispers over my skin, easing the burn of the sun as Neal steers the boat out of its slip and starts across the lake. It couldn't be a more beautiful day for this and I can't wipe the smile from my face while I watch all the activity around us.

The lake hosts a lot of fisherman, people on jetskis, and an array of boats I have no names for. "We'll drive around a little and find a quiet place," Neal says.

If I wasn't already a hundred percent in love and lust with this man, seeing him like this would do it. Stripped down to nothing but a pair of shorts, he guides the boat with such confidence, a serene smile planted on his lips. He looks right at home.

The sun makes his blue green eyes shine and the wind whips his wavy hair around, making me want to run my hands through it. "You look so damn sexy right now," I announce, and his smile expands. Steering us to a little cove, he kills the engine. We're far enough away from the other boaters and people that we can hear the sound of the waves lapping at the boat. A woodpecker hammers away in the forest nearby, and dragonflies hum over our heads.

Lying back on the cushioned bench, I breathe, "It's like paradise."

"Wait until tonight, when the stars come out," he says, taking a seat on the deck and leaning his back against the bench. He turns his head and I capture his lips with mine. They're soft and warmed by the sun. The usual desperate, passionate frenzy that always exists when we come together isn't present. This is different. It's a leisurely, sweet kiss that makes my heart swell with emotions I've tried not to feel.

When we part, I press another soft kiss against his bottom lip and murmur, "I love you."

His fingers thread through my hair and his gaze locks on mine. "I love you, V." He shifts and slips his hand into mine. "You haven't said anything, but I know moving in together makes you nervous. I'm sure it'll take some adjustment on everyone's part, but I swear, we'll make it work."

"I know." I sit up and slide down to sit beside him. "It just feels a little too good to be true sometimes."

"Moving in together?"

"I always wanted a family. It was always just me and mom, and, well...you've met her. Then I thought I had a chance at it with Clint, which was a huge mistake. Well, not completely, because I had Aiden, but now he's growing up the same way, with only me for support."

"Not anymore," he says. "I'll treat him like my own. We'll be a family. Even if you never agree to marry me."

Chuckling, I look up at him. "Is that really what you want?"

"Yes." There's no hesitation in his response. "But only when I know you want it too."

"It's not you. I just...never saw the point in marriage. It's a bit creepy. It's like, I love you so much I'm going to get the government involved so you can't leave."

He throws his head back and his laugh echoes over the lake. "That's one way to look at it."

"How do you see it?"

"Marriage is standing in front of everyone you care about and telling the world that this is the person you want to be with forever. It's not swearing to the government, or a god, or even those watching, but to each other. Then, when the hard times come and there are days you might worry that it's all falling apart, you can remember that oath and know the other person isn't going anywhere. That trouble will pass, and love will still be there."

"Even though divorce exists?"

"So does death, but you don't spend your life anticipating it."

We're quiet for a few moments as I mull over his words. A sudden squeal from a woman on a passing boat breaks the silence. "A year," I murmur.

"What?"

"Once we've lived together a year, if you want to get

married, I'm willing."

A smile leaps across his face. "I'm holding you to that."

A bead of sweat runs down my side, and I stand up, stripping off my shirt and shorts to reveal the bikini underneath. "Go for a swim with me?"

I don't have to ask him twice.

We sit cuddled together, watching the descending sun throw a million sparkles over the water, putting an end to one of the best days of my life. One of those I know I'll always remember.

Goosebumps race across my skin, and Neal kisses my neck as I shiver. "Come on, let's go dry off and put some clothes on."

While we're getting changed, Aiden calls to say goodnight, and I put him on speakerphone.

"Can I stay up another hour?" he begs.

"What did Noble say?"

"That there's only so much fun he can take in one night, but that don't make sense! Fun is good!"

"So is sleep. So be good and go to bed. I love you."

"Fine," he grumbles. "Love you too."

"Let me talk to Noble."

There's some scrambling around before Noble says, "Hey."

"Hey, everything going okay?"

"Yeah, they're fine. Except Aiden broke the soap dish off the shower wall, and I have no clue how that happened. Something about Spiderman. Your boy could turn a rock inside out."

Neal smiles at me as he pulls out a blanket. "So, you've had too much fun?"

"Oh yeah. I just listened to a ten-minute argument because Bailey asked him 'What rhymes with door?' and he said 'No, it doesn't.'"

Neal and I both crack up.

"But everything's good. They're going to bed now, and I'm calling to get a vasectomy."

I hear Aiden pipe up in the background. "Is that a video game? I want to play vasectomy!"

"Did you do a lot of drugs when you were pregnant?" Noble asks. "I'm not judging."

"Good night, Noble. Thanks again," I laugh.

Neal and I are still chuckling over Aiden and Noble when we make our way back up onto the deck. My laughter is cut short when I'm struck by the beauty of the world that seems to have transformed over the last half hour.

In the distance, I can see the lights of a few other boats, but we're too far away to hear anything but the sounds of nature around us. The wind has died down and the night is warm and fragrant with the scent of the forest around us.

The true magic of the scene though, comes from the sky. Stars burst across it, closer, clearer, and in greater numbers than I've ever seen. The calm water reflects them, making it hard to tell which way is up.

Neal sets a battery-operated lantern beside the foam mat he's already spread out on the deck, but doesn't turn it on. While I marvel at our surroundings, he goes below, returns with pillows and a blanket, and makes us a cozy spot to relax.

Stretching out, he pulls me down beside him and we stare at the sky. I could stay right here forever. "It's so beautiful. You can even see the milky way."

"I loved spending the night on a boat when I was a kid. My parents would sleep in the hull and I'd sleep under the stars."

I cuddle up to him, pressing my cheek to his chest. "Did you ever get woken up by rain?"

"No, but a bird shit on me once, right in my hair. I slept through it, but my dad's laughter woke me up."

"Are you serious?"

He grins down at me. "Absolutely. I was mad because he made me get up and jump in the lake to wash it off. It was freezing, and I was still half asleep."

He stops my giggle with a soft kiss. Our lips part for a

second, and our eyes meet, before we kiss again, and his hands wander over my body. There's no urgency this time, no desperation to get all we can of the other because we have limited time, or the kids might catch us, but the passion is overpowering as always.

Our clothing ends up piled at our feet, and I close my eyes at the foreign sensation of the night air blowing across my naked body. It's exhilarating because it feels like we're out in the open, but we can't actually be seen or heard by any of the other boaters in the distance.

When he slides inside me with a tenderness I've not felt before, my head tilts back, and a quiet moan escapes. We aren't fucking this time. He makes love to me—slow, steady, mind blowing love—while the stars shine down on us and the boat rocks with our joined bodies.

We roll over, and I ride him at the same pace, bending over to kiss the rasp of his stubble covered jaw. He sits up and wraps his arms around me. Moving together for what feels like hours, we both slowly build until we come together, my face buried in his neck. I don't know how long we lie there after, cuddled together, watching the stars nightly journey across the sky, but it's the most peaceful thing I've ever experienced.

A drop in temperature finally chases us inside where we curl up in bed together. Maybe it was the sun, the swimming, or the sex, but exhaustion sends me to sleep almost immediately. I awake once in the middle of the night to hear the steady beat of rain above us. It wakes Neal as well, and without moving from his position behind me, he silently slips inside me again. The sound of the rain, the rocking of the boat, and another slow, devastating orgasm puts me right back out.

In the morning, I'm not sure how much of my memory is true and what was a dream, it was all so perfect.

Chapter Fifteen

Neal

"Over here, buddy!" I call to Aiden, and he pulls his wagon over to me. It's full of items that Veronica is selling in the yard sale.

"Mom said she'll be over in a minute," he says, wiping his little forehead.

Nine o'clock in the morning and it's already ninety degrees, with enough humidity to drown in the air. We'll be lucky if people still show up with the heat advisories in place. We really should've checked the weather before having a yard sale, but it doesn't matter much. At this time of year, it's either boil your balls hot or raining.

My little entrepreneur is taking advantage of the situation. Bailey has spent her allowance, plus some money she had saved, on cases of drinks and a few boxes of popsicles. The popsicles are in the freezer inside, but the cooler is full of ice cold drinks she plans to sell. Darla loaned her a big sun umbrella that she's driven into the ground to sit under, and Aiden joins her.

Two cars pull up just as Veronica joins me, but I barely notice them. I'm used to seeing Veronica in a t-shirt and shorts or completely naked. There hasn't been much in-between, but her outfit today turns me into a staring idiot. Her tiny cotton shorts stop just below her ass cheeks, and a halter top leaves her abdomen bare. Blissfully unaware of my gawking and the stare of one of the men who exits the car parked behind her, she makes her way over to me.

"Shit, it's hot already. Bailey had a good idea with the drinks."

"Uh-huh." Yeah, still staring as she bends over to rifle through a box of books.

She looks up at me, blinking at the sun in her eyes. "Are you okay?"

"Yeah, I'm good." Christ, Neal, get it together. You're not a damn teenager.

A minivan pulls up and two women get out, along with two young kids. "Mom! They got popsicles! I want a popsicle!"

Rolling her eyes, one of the women brings the kids over to purchase popsicles from Bailey, along with two bottles of water. Yeah, she's going to make a killing today. Bailey sends Aiden in for the popsicles, and he happily obliges. He's stuck like glue to her today because she'll be leaving to spend some time at my parents' soon and he's not happy about it.

The sale goes better than I anticipated. Even after everything we gave to charity and threw away, we have a ton of stuff to sell. As the day grows hotter, the steady stream of customers becomes a trickle.

The Frat Hell guys and their friends stop by and all six of them buy a drink from Bailey, leaving her with a giant smile on her face. The only other customers are a woman who has three boys around twelve or thirteen with her. They all browse around, but the boys spend their time digging through a box under one of the tables, giggling and exclaiming over whatever they've found.

I can't remember what's in it. Probably books or DVD's. I think Bailey set that one out. Veronica notices them as well when loud laughter erupts, followed by a shriek from one of the ladies.

What the hell? Did a mouse climb in the box or something? That's really my only thought as I start across the yard.

The lady who screamed grabs one of the boys by the arm and shouts, "In the car! Now!" They all hustle toward the car, and she scowls at me as she passes, hissing, "You should be ashamed of yourself! Deviant pervert!"

The Frat Hell guys practically sprint to see what's in the box and beat me there by a few steps.

Oh fuck.

I'm never going to live this down.

The cardboard box may look like any other, but it has sealed my fate as the neighborhood pervert.

Bailey starts toward us, but Veronica stops her, and sends her and Aiden down to Jani's to get more bags. It's a good thing.

No daughter should ever see her father's high school porn collection.

I don't know why I kept it. There are magazines and VHS tapes in that box that are almost twenty years old. Dating back before you could just jump on the internet and see whatever you want.

By the time I try to yank the box up, the guys have already dragged out videos with titles like *Anustasia, Bend Over Like Beckham,* and *Sorest Rump*.

Noble sits back on the grass, holding a magazine bearing the headline *Sir Cumsalot Spanks a Wench*, laughing and trying to talk. "You'd better…be careful, Veronica…I see…a pattern."

Fuck.

"Dude, I knew you were old, but…magazines?" Denton snorts, and all the guys burst out laughing again.

I'm still trying to find a way out of this when another car pulls up, and a guy with a kid gets out. Noble tosses a ten-dollar bill at me and snatches up the box. "I'll just get this out of your way. Worth every penny," he laughs as the group starts down the road back to the Frat Hell apartment.

"A lot of spanking mags in here, Veronica," Denton taunts as he passes by her. "Better be good."

She slaps him on the arm, and he cracks up.

Great. I can't stop them without calling attention to what they're laughing about so they're going to take them home and see every crazy fetish magazine and porno I managed to get my hands on as a teenager.

Perfect.

Veronica doesn't say anything to me as the man and little boy pick out and purchase a few of Aiden's old toys. The smirk on her lips every time she looks at me doesn't feel like a good sign though.

Finally, we're alone, and she approaches me, laughter breaking through her words, "So, I guess you're an ass man?"

Her giggles break the stern expression I was trying to maintain. "I've had those since I was thirteen. I forgot I even had them. Bailey must've set them out when she moved the DVD boxes from my closet."

"So, I don't have to worry you'll go all Fifty Shades on me and throw me over your knee?"

I had an ex that was into spanking, and as much as I fantasized about it when I was young, it's not really my thing, but now the visual is in my head and all I want to do is put her plump ass in the air. "Depends on whether you bring this up again."

"I have an idea. You never say the words 'fucking idiot' again and I'll pretend this never happened."

Laughing, I wrap my arms around her and drop a kiss on her lips. "Deal."

"We're a mess," she laughs.

"Makes us perfect together."

"Do you want me to go get your box of teenage deviance away from the guys?"

"Only if you burn it."

"Deal. You can clean up," she says, gesturing to the remnants of the yard sale.

Sighing, I start gathering the leftover items to take to the thrift shop. I guess I shouldn't really be concerned. Half the neighborhood saw me running home in what appeared to be shit stained underwear. What's a few pornos compared to that?

I figured the Frat Hell guys would bring up the porno thing for a while, then grow bored of it. I should've known better. Every day since the yard sale, I've found a page hidden somewhere. Under the visor in my car, tucked in my barbecue grill, taped to the inside of the lid of my outdoor trash can. At least they've made sure to put them where I'll find them and not Bailey. Still, when I open a piece of junk mail and find an ad for a spanking bench alongside the pre-approval for a credit card, I know this won't blow over anytime soon. College kids have too much time on their hands in the summer.

Veronica is a ball of nerves and it's so adorable. My parents are coming today to pick up Bailey for their usual summer visit and I swear, she has changed clothes three times, like maybe they'd like her better in a blue shirt instead of red.

"Relax, V," I pull her down beside me on the couch and wrap my arm around her. "They are going to love you."

"Do they know about me?"

"Of course. The last time I visited, my dad said we were both dumbasses for keeping things distant because of the kids. I guess I'm going to have to admit he was right."

The corners of her mouth tilt up as she peeks up at me. "They knew we were seeing each other before?"

I run my fingers down her arm. "I knew then I wanted more. I wanted to wait until after we moved to say anything because I thought it'd be easier on Bailey, not to have so much to adjust to at once. But this was always going to happen, V."

She lays her head on my shoulder and picks up my hand. She always loves playing with my hands. "I'm glad you didn't wait."

"Me too."

"They're here!" Bailey crows, darting through the front door.

Veronica swallows and takes a deep breath. Chuckling, I pull her to her feet and we head outside. "Come on. Time to let my mother fawn all over you while my father embarrasses me."

Mom and Dad are barely out of the car before Bailey is blathering away to them, telling them all about the new house and how Veronica and Aiden are moving in with us. I hadn't really mentioned that yet.

"Mom, Dad, this is Veronica, and her son, Aiden."

"Moving in together?" Mom says, her face lighting up as she stoops down to talk to Aiden. "Hi, it's nice to meet you."

Aiden smiles at her. "I can ride a bike with no training wheels. Neal taught me. Want to see?"

"Ade," Veronica lays a hand on his shoulder. "Not right now. Let them come in. They've had a long drive." She smiles at Mom. "It's nice to meet you..."

"Holly, and this old man is Charles," Mom says before she grabs her in a hug. "I'm so happy to meet you! Neal has told me so much about you and your little boy. And Aiden is all Bailey talks about. But I didn't know you were going to be living together. You have to tell me all about yourself!"

Dad grins at me and slaps me on the back as we walk toward Veronica's apartment. "Looks like you pulled your head out of your ass. She's a beauty. Got to watch those redheads though. They have those fiery tempers."

"I'll keep that in mind."

"You'll have to excuse the mess. We've all been staying here while we get the house ready," Veronica says. "Only a few more weeks and we'll be out of here."

After an hour or so of conversation and laughter, Veronica gives me a smile filled with relief. I hope she's seeing the same thing I am. We can do this. We can make a family.

My parents only stay a couple of hours since they have such a long drive back. It's the first time I've seen Bailey hesitate or seem upset about going home with them.

I give her a big hug and reassure her, "Have fun. We'll all be moving into the house by the time you get back."

Aiden bursts into tears when she gets ready to leave and she hugs him. "It's not for long and then you'll have a room right across from mine. We can read a story every night," she promises him.

"Even if it's the dino babies story that Mom said she'd rather run naked through a herd of porcupines than read again?" he says with a sniffle.

Veronica covers her smile and shakes her head while my parents try to hide their chuckles.

"Even that one."

"'Kay."

We watch them pull out of the parking lot, then Aiden turns to me. "Is my room really across from Bailey's?"

"It sure is." I wink at Veronica. "The place is a mess right now, but we can go and see it if you want. I need to know what color to paint your room."

Aiden's eyes light up. "I can pick?"

"Within reason," Veronica inserts.

Yeah, she knew where he'd run with this. "I want blue and red stripes! No, the whole room black with those sticky yellow stars! No, wait…"

Laughing at his excited suggestions, we climb into Veronica's car to show Aiden the new house.

I'm spending most of my free time at the new place, but Veronica has only been in here once. Since it's not safe for the kids, she usually keeps them while I get the carpentry and other work finished. I have a little surprise for her in the kitchen and I can't wait for her to see it. It's one of the things she complains about not having in her apartment.

Once we get inside, Veronica heads to one of the bathrooms she's been working on, to check the measurements for some curtains, and I take Aiden upstairs.

"It's dusty here," he says, waving a hand in front of his face.

"Yeah, it's pretty dirty, but we're going to fix it up like new." I open the door to what will be his room. "This will be your room."

He walks inside and a grin spreads across his face. "It's big!"

It's twice the size of his tiny bedroom at home. I walk over to one wall. 'See, we can put your bed here, your dresser and desk over there, and you'll have a big space to play with your toys."

"And my cars will roll! No carpet!" he announces gleefully. Staring around the room, he says, "Can the walls be red? Eddie says red is a girl color, but I like it."

"There are no girl or boy colors. What kind of red? Like

your shoes?" I ask, touching his bright red sneakers with my foot.

"Like a firetruck." His eyes widen. "And I have a poster of a firetruck!"

"Do you want a firetruck room?" Just a few days ago, I saw a unique set of bunk beds that were made to look like a fire engine at a local flea market. They need some work, but it's nothing I can't do.

"Yes!" He dances around like he always does when he's happy.

"Sounds good to me, buddy. Let's run it by your mom."

Veronica's voice filters up through the floor vent in Aiden's room. "Neal! Oh my god! Are you serious?" I guess she found her surprise.

"Come on. Let's go tell her."

On the way back downstairs, I show him where Bailey's room is, right across the hall from him, and the master bedroom where Veronica and I will stay. "Do you like the house?"

"Yes! Can we move right now?"

Laughing, I lead him through the living room. "Not until I fix the place up, but it won't be long."

His gaze catches the expansive backyard through the window. "Can I go see the backyard?"

"Sure, stay inside the fence, though."

He darts outside, and I walk into the kitchen to see Veronica crouched down, reading the back of the large box. Her face is pure happiness when she looks up at me. "You bought a dishwasher?"

"I did. Sorry, I know how much you loved washing by hand, but this just seemed more sanitary."

She tackles me in a hug and drops a kiss on my lips. "You don't hate hand washing. I know you got this for me. Thank you."

I tighten my arms around her, and quickly glance around to make sure Aiden is still outside. "The less time you're in here, the more time you're in my bed. Or bent over it."

She chuckles and steps back to admire the box again. "As long as you aren't paddling me."

"Oh, not you too," I groan.

"Well, I found a big plastic paddle on my car seat this morning."

"Fucking Frat Hell," I murmur.

Aiden flies in through the back door. "I smashed a ginormous anthill! This place is awesome! I want to live here forever!" He runs back outside.

Veronica smiles after him. "Well, we have his seal of approval."

Veronica and I haven't spent much time together lately. She has been working more since it's the hotel's busy season, and my time has been split between work and remodeling the house. Our days are long, and we both fall into bed at night, exhausted.

It's early on Sunday morning when I get woken by a phone call from the lawyer who is trying to help put a stop to the multitude of offenses committed by the Violent Circle management. A call on a Sunday morning seems a bit foreboding, but it turns out to be good news.

"Neal, I have some news. Since Orchid Apartments are funded partially by the Federal Housing Department, they were also served papers with your complaints, and they plan to investigate. Are there tenants who would be willing to talk to them?"

"Yes, I'm sure they would. I have copies of the most recent threat letters as well, that I can share with them."

"Good. We need to pull no punches here. If they find enough violations, they'll pull the management back in line. They won't risk losing federal funding. There's no way that place survives without it."

"Okay, tell me what I need to do."

"They plan to show up for a surprise inspection tomorrow. They'll go door to door, inspecting apartments and asking the tenants about how they've been treated. First, you should let your neighbors know what's coming. Make sure they understand they aren't there to judge their housekeeping like the previous inspections carried out by the management. They want to see that the units are up to code, and livable. The more the tenants cooperate, the better the chance of the department intervening and helping your cause."

"Second, I was contacted by a young man named Noble Bradley about the local news station covering this story. I think now would be the best time. It should get the public on our side and put even more pressure on them. Do you think the neighborhood would react favorably to be interviewed on camera?"

"Some of them," I reply, hesitating a bit. "You have to understand that some of these people will be homeless if this doesn't go our way and the management decides to retaliate against the whistleblowers."

"I do understand. I'd suggest getting together a list of those willing to talk to the reporters and informing the station. But when it comes to the inspectors, please try to get as many people as possible to tell the truth about the daily struggles there. I've been assured, the questions won't be asked with any member of management present, nor will the answers be shared with them."

"I understand. I'll get on it."

Veronica lies beside me and she cuddles up to me when I hang up the phone. "Is everything okay?"

"The shit is about to hit the fan."

After I explain everything to her, she climbs out of bed and starts getting dressed. "Everyone needs to get their places clean and neat, though. The more responsible we look, the more we'll be believed. I'll call Emily and warn her."

"I'm going to talk to Noble and see if WFUK is still interested in the story. Then I'll make sure everyone knows what's up."

Veronica shakes her head. "I'm sorry I have to work today, or I'd help."

I plant a kiss on her lips. "I've got it covered."

The next two days are stressful, but hopefully, it'll be

worth it. I was surprised how many tenants are more than willing to talk to the reporter, along with the inspectors. The inspectors show up first, and after only a few apartments, it's easy to tell they aren't happy.

"You received this letter because your child drew a hopscotch on the sidewalk?" one of the inspectors asks, to clarify.

"Yes. Freida also stopped my daughter to tell her that she would get her family kicked out if she did it again."

"And how old is your daughter?"

"Seven."

It goes on like that for each apartment, and I look up to see the news van rolling in just as the inspectors finish the last apartment. The reporter asks one of them a few questions, but she keeps her answers brief.

"A few complaints have been filed about the living conditions here, so we've launched an investigation. I can't comment any further on the matter."

The tenants can though.

The reporter spends over an hour listening to tales of the inspections, the draconian rules, the threats made to our children and us. I don't know how much will actually make the news once it's edited down, but I have no doubt it will make an impact.

Chapter Sixteen

Veronica

The last few weeks have flown by. We're still waiting to hear from the housing management, and everyone has been on edge waiting for them to retaliate on the scathing piece the local news station aired a few days after the surprise inspections. Since that day, there hasn't been one threat letter placed on anyone's door, and they've been scrambling to make repairs that should've been made long ago.

None of this is really going to affect us now, since we've just finished moving our things into our new place. We're officially free of Violent Circle, but that doesn't mean we don't still care about our friends and neighbors still living there.

Noble, Jani, and Emily have teamed up to throw us a goodbye party, and I'm looking forward to one last, crazy night on the Circle. Aiden barely listens when I tell him he'll be staying with Neal's parents tonight. He's glued to the step, watching for them to bring Bailey home.

"Bailey!" Aiden yells and runs to hug her, almost knocking her over.

Laughing, she hugs him, then kneels to open her backpack. "I got you something at the zoo." Aiden's eyes light up at the plastic hippo she produces.

"A hippo! And its mouth opens! It can eat people!" He

makes chomping sounds, opening and closing its mouth on Bailey's arm, making her giggle. Grabbing her arm, he pulls her toward the house. "Come and see your room!"

They disappear inside, and Holly laughs, hugging me. "What I'd give to have half that energy," she says.

Charles approaches behind her, carrying their suitcases, and Neal grabs one from him. "We don't have all the work done yet, but the house is coming together," he says, as they follow us inside.

We give them a tour, and they ooh and ahh over everything, admiring the work we've done. Holly and I lose Charles and Neal when we start going room to room, talking about décor. I'm not that great at decorating, so I'm not going to miss a chance to pick her brain for ideas and opinions.

"I was thinking yellow for the kitchen," I tell her.

"Oh, I just saw the most beautiful sunflower print curtains that would look amazing in here." She pulls out her phone and shows me a picture.

Neal winks at me as he and his dad settle in the living room.

"Would you like a cup of coffee?" I ask Holly, and she accepts. We sit at the kitchen table chatting and laughing. It's amazing how easy she is to talk to, and I envy Neal for growing up with a mother like her.

"So, we're watching the kids tonight?" she says, sipping her coffee.

"Only if you don't mind. Violent Circle is throwing us a going away party." I chuckle. "They take any chance to throw a party."

Holly grins at me over her cup. "Would you be okay with leaving the kids with Charles?"

I sit back, confused. "Of course, if you have something you'd like to do or if you aren't feeling up to it—"

"Oh no, dear. I want to go with you. I can't remember the last time I went to a good party. Charles can be such a stick in the mud."

Oh hell. She has no idea what she'll be walking into. "Uh, you're welcome to come, of course, but…their parties can get pretty crazy."

A gleam appears in her eye as she replies, "So can I."

Neal isn't going to like this, but he'll get over it. She deserves to get out and have fun, too. "All right, then. Do you want to go shopping for a costume? The psychos have decided to have a Halloween party in the summer."

"What are you going as?"

Sighing, I finish off my drink. "Your son chose our costumes." I get to my feet. "Come on, I'll show you."

When I told Neal he could choose whatever couples costume he wanted, I expected some cartoon characters or zombies or something. But, really, who could have predicted he'd come back with an electrical outlet costume for me and a plug for him. The costumes fit together, but showing his mother that his prongs go in the ass of my outlet costume was uncomfortable at best. Though she finds it hilarious.

"Oh lord. You can't let him choose in the future. He once dressed up as a condom when he was a teenager. My boy's not normal," she laughs.

"That's okay. Neither am I." I put the costumes away and turn to her. "There's a costume shop in the next town, about half an hour away."

"Let's go." Her excitement is adorable.

I peek my head into the living room while she fetches her purse. "Neal? Watch the kids for an hour or so?"

"Sure, where are you going?"

"I'm taking your mom to find a costume. She's going to the party with us tonight."

Neal's mouth drops open, and his father's laughter follows us out the door.

Holly is so much fun to hang out with. We spend over an hour in the costume store, trying on different things until she settles on what she wants. On the way home, we stop and pick up dinner at a fast food chicken place, so no one has to cook.

"What did you get?" Charles asks when we return.

"You'll see," she taunts him.

"Woman if you come out here in booty shorts with your

hooters hanging out, we're going to have problems!" Charles calls as she carries the bags to the guest room.

The kids and I die laughing, especially because Neal looks like he wants to climb under the couch.

"What are booty shorts?" Bailey asks, and Aiden quickly follows that with "What are hooters?"

"Owls," Bailey replies, making everyone laugh again. She gets on her phone, and I know she's looking up booty shorts. A second later she heads upstairs to the guest room. "Grandma! You don't really have those shorts, do you?"

Neal moves to sit beside me on the couch. "V, tell me my mother isn't going to come out of there dressed like a slutty butterfly or something."

Cuddling against him, I press a kiss to his stubbly jaw. "Relax, it's not revealing."

"Thank fuck."

"And she really liked our ass socket costume you picked."

Groaning, he lays his head back. "In no world, did I imagine she'd be present when we wore that. I can't believe you invited her to the party."

"She wanted to get out and have some fun. I warned her what it will be like. She'll be fine." I grin up at him. "I really like your mom. Your dad too."

He kisses my ear before murmuring, "Someday, I hope they'll be your in-laws. You just have to let me know when we need to get the government involved."

I can't help but laugh as he repeats the words I chose to describe my view on marriage. "I love you," I whisper, planting a quick kiss on his lips.

"Love you too."

"I love it, Grandma!" Bailey's squeal travels downstairs. "It's so funny!"

"Just remember taking Mom was your idea," he adds, covering his eyes with his palm.

"Relax." I pat his stomach. "It'll be fine."

A few hours later finds us standing in the living room in our costumes, waiting for Holly to come out of the guest room.

A thump followed by footsteps can be heard from the hall. Again and again. Thump, step step. Thump, step step. I can't fight back my smile at the confusion on Neal and Charles's face until Holly steps through the doorway.

They both burst into laughter at her "queen of the nursing home" costume, and a smile breaks across her face.

She thumps the walker forward again and hobbles into the room. Saggy hose hangs just under her knees where her ratty robe ends. Her gray wig has a few stray pink curlers attached that bob as she walks. Dark framed glasses hang around her neck on a chain, and her comically big handbag rests at her waist. Yeah, there's a bottle of Schnapps in that bag. She had me stop at the liquor store on the way back.

"I love it!" Neal laughs, hugging her. I can hear the relief in his voice that she didn't wear something revealing. There's no way I'm giving away what's under that robe. I don't want to miss his face when he sees.

She's not going to do it now though. "I'm ready when you whipper snappers are," she says in a frail voice.

"See," I laugh, grabbing Neal's arm on the way to the car. "This will be fun."

Violent Circle has lost its mind.

When we pull in, Neal bursts out laughing.

There's a giant bounce house set up in the middle of the basketball court. That isn't all. There's a climbing wall, a massive inflatable waterslide that ends in a pool a few feet deep, and I shit you not, a mechanical bull, surrounded by an inflatable wall. All set up side by side around the playground.

Throngs of people—of adults—are clambering over the equipment, hooting and hollering as they race down the slide or get tossed off the bull. This isn't a party. It's a kiddie carnival.

"What the hell?" Neal says as we get out of the car.

"Isn't it great?" Denton exclaims. He's wearing a giant hot dog costume. "Kenny got a job at the party store, so he got to borrow all this stuff for free!"

"I thought you said no kids," I point out.

Denton looks around. "Do you see any kids? We let them play on it until a half hour ago. Now it's our turn. Keg is beside the laundry room." He turns his focus to Holly. "And who is this?"

"This is my mom, Holly. Mom, this is Denton."

Denton cracks up. "I love your costume."

"And I love yours. Nothing better than a big wiener."

Denton laughs and gestures for her to follow him. "I already like you better than your son. Can I get you a drink?"

Holly digs in her big handbag and pulls out a fifth of schnapps. "I could use a glass and some ice, if you don't mind."

Despite his reluctance to bring her along, Neal's lips tilt up, and he looks at me. "We're going to be carrying her home."

Holly holds her own though, and we only see her here and there as she bounces around the party, making friends out of whoever she talks to. Neal relaxes a bit, and as we both down the drinks, the night really starts to get fun.

"Hey!" Noble yells, pointing to the waterslide. "Come on!"

"I'll get electrocuted!" I shout back.

Holly heads up the slide, and everyone cheers. Even Neal grins at her, waiting on her to splash down into the pool. She stands at the top of the slide and soaks in the hoots and cheers of the crowd.

I know what she's about to do before she does it.

Neal is going to shit.

"Check me out, boys!" she shouts and throws open the robe to reveal the best part of her costume. The flesh colored body suit with fake boobs that hang almost to her knees is just as funny the second time I see it, especially when the boobs swing, revealing the mini afro of dark black hair glued to the crotch.

Everyone loses it, laughing, pointing, and there is more than one person recording on their phone when she seat drops onto the slide. She splashes into the pool at the bottom. Neal and Noble rush to help her out of the water, since the costume has now become a weight.

"Jesus, Mom," Neal laughs. "I can't take you anywhere."

Jani approaches, still laughing. "Holly, we can walk down to my apartment if you want to borrow some clothes. You look about my size."

"That would be lovely," Holly agrees. She grabs the boobs that are now hanging well past her knees, rings them out, and tosses one over each shoulder. "I'm ready. This has been the best party."

"Just wait until the strippers show up," Jani jokes, and they head toward her apartment.

Neal chugs his beer. 'You don't really think she hired strippers, do you?"

"Nah, it's not a bachelorette party."

Neither Neal nor I want to get wet, but we do take a turn in the bounce house, and on the mechanical bull. Holly waves at us from across the park, now dressed in jeans and T-shirt, and I give her a thumbs up.

It's well after midnight and the party shows no sign of breaking up. I feel a little sorry for the residents who have kids because there's little chance anyone is sleeping through this. If there's one thing Violent Circle knows how to do, it's throw a party.

I'm having a fantastic time, though the alcohol is starting to hit me hard. "Jani! I'm going to use your bathroom!" I call to her, and she nods.

"I'm coming with," Holly tells me. "Schnapps goes right through me."

Noble and a few other guys are hanging out in Jani's living room, playing a drinking game, but they pay us no mind as we take turns in her bathroom. Just as I'm joining everyone in the living room, there's a knock on the door.

"It's cops!" Noble calls.

"Oh shit, Jani really did hire strippers," I announce.

Noble rolls his eyes. "Of course she did."

"Open up! We need to talk!" one of them shouts.

Noble chuckles and yells back. "There are three of you! Talk to each other!"

Laughing, I open the door, and Holly's face lights up. She grins at me before approaching them. "Hel-lo officers, wow, I have broken so many laws tonight. Just whip those handcuffs out now."

The older guy—he's maybe thirty-five—keeps a stern expression and steps back as she runs her hand down his chest. "Ma'am, we've had a noise complaint. It's clear you're having some kind of celebration tonight, but it's time to wrap it up."

These guys are good. But they aren't dancing.

My vision wavers a bit as I pull out my phone and turn on some music. "Okay, let's see it! Shake it, guys! I got dollars!"

Holly and I both start dancing, but she's rubbing all over the older guy, so I focus on one of the younger ones. I'm sure Neal wouldn't mind if I had a quick dance with him, right?

"Ma'am!" he stutters, when I sidle up against him. "You need to step back."

"What? No touching? Do I need to pay extra for that?" I reach out to stroke his bicep, and he catches my wrist. At the same time, the older guy spins Holly around and cuffs her hands behind her back.

"Whew, that's what I'm talking about," she says.

The young officer repeats the action with me. Cold metal circles my wrists, and I giggle. "Don't put anything in my back socket. That's reserved for my boyfriend."

One of them snorts out a laugh.

I never realized just how out of touch with reality alcohol can render a person until we're being lead out to two waiting police cars. Maybe it's the cool night air sobering me a bit or the jaws dropping all around us as we're tucked into the back of the police car.

"Veronica," Holly whispers, her eyes wide.

"Yeah."

"I don't think they're strippers."

The street light shines through the window illuminating her face, and our gazes meet for a second before we both crack up. "We're in so much trouble," I giggle.

"Charles will never let me hear the end of this."

"Neal is going to kill me."

Neal, Noble, and a ton of others are trying to talk the cops into letting us go, explaining the mistake, but it does no good. A few seconds later, we're on our way to jail.

Chapter Seventeen

Neal

Ten minutes. Veronica and mom were away from me for ten minutes and they got themselves arrested.

"This is my fault!" Jani exclaims as the squad cars drive away. "I was just teasing about strippers."

"What did they do?" I ask Noble.

"They thought the cops were strippers, so they tried to dance with them."

"That's all?" I ask skeptically.

"Your mother may have grabbed one of the officer's ass, but, I swear, Veronica only felt his bicep."

There's some general laughter, and I can't blame them. If it were anyone else this would be funny as hell.

"Is anyone sober?" I ask, and Mitch steps forward.

"Yeah, I can't drink. Doc's got me on some pills that can't be mixed with alcohol or they fry your liver."

"He's got that little Lamisil monster living in his shoe," someone shouts, and he turns to flip them off. "I can drive you down to the jail."

"If you can take me home, I'd appreciate it. Dad can run to the jail with me."

"I'm sure once you explain, everything will be fine," Darla speaks up, peeking out from under her big sun hat.

"I'm coming with you!" Jani exclaims. "I can tell them I'm the one who said I ordered strippers."

"I'll stay with the kids," Noble laughs, joining us.

We all climb into Mitch's car, and he drops us off at my house. I can't think of anything I'd rather do less than tell Dad where his wife is at this moment, but there's no help for it.

Dad and Bailey both look up when we enter. They're sitting on the couch, Bailey with her guitar on her lap. Aiden plays with his new toy hippo on the floor.

"What's wrong?" Dad says.

"Uh, let's talk upstairs."

Bailey casts a worried look at me, and I give her a reassuring smile. "Everything's fine. No one is hurt."

She doesn't quite look like she believes me, but she nods.

Noble sits on the floor with Aiden, keeping him occupied.

Dad and Jani follow me upstairs. There wasn't much point explaining things away from the kids when his voice booms through the house. "Arrested! Your mother was arrested? For what?"

"Feeling up a cop she thought was a stripper," Jani blurts when I hesitate. "It was totally my fault. I'm going to explain everything to them."

Dad rubs his face and coughs out a laugh. "For fuck's sake, Holly," he mumbles. "Okay, let's go get them."

I hope it's that easy. If we can't convince them it was all a terrible mistake, they'll probably keep them until they go in front of a judge tomorrow.

Fortunately, the two officers on duty at the station know me pretty well. I've helped them get Barney, our resident alcoholic, back into his apartment a time or two and they generally stop to chat when they pass by.

"Officer Green," I greet him, approaching the desk. He takes one look at my plug costume and his chest shakes with laughter.

"Are you missing an outlet, there, Neal?"

"There's been a misunderstanding."

"That's what I hear." Chuckling, he gets to his feet.

Jani rushes up to him. "It was my fault. I told her there were strippers coming and when the officers showed up, Veronica and Holly thought they were strippers in costume. They didn't mean to...manhandle the officers."

Officer Green laughs and wipes his eyes. Waving to us, he says, "Come on back."

It's a tiny station with two holding cells, usually reserved for the few drunk and disorderly offenders that are picked up. Anyone who is a true threat is sent to the bigger annex run by the staties.

Mom sits back on the bench, her ankles crossed like she's lounging at home, and laughs at something Veronica says.

"They aren't exactly remorseful," Officer Green snorts.

Veronica struggles to her feet in her outlet costume. "We apologized to all three officers. And explained what happened."

"You can't charge us with public intox," Holly insists. "We were inside. You dragged us out into public."

Officer Green turns to me and Dad, shaking his head. "Are you sure you want them back?"

"Somebody's got to make breakfast," Dad replies, relaxing now that he sees they aren't going to keep them.

"Are you pressing charges?" I ask.

Officer Green opens the cell door. "No, you all gave me a new story to tell. Get their asses out of here."

"Thank you." I shake his hand as Mom and Veronica step out into the hall.

"Do you have anything to say for yourself?" Dad asks.

Mom flips her hair back and lays a hand on her stomach. "I'm starving. Is the Breakfast Hut still open?"

Veronica cracks up laughing, and I hook an arm around her neck, pulling her against me. "What's this I hear about you feeling up his bicep?"

"Me?" she scoffs, grinning. "Do I look like I'd do something so immature?"

As we make our way out of the station, one of the officers that brought them in walks past and nods to us. He's barely out of earshot before mom announces, "Firm ass on that one. They must make them run a lot."

When we get to the parking lot, I call Noble, who assures me the kids are fine. Mom and Veronica are still going on about breakfast, and Noble mentions the kids are hungry. Fuck it. "Have them put their shoes on. We're going to go to the Breakfast Hut. Do you want to go?"

"No thanks. I want to get back to the party." He tells the kids, and I can hear them cheer.

What the hell, it's summer. One late night won't hurt them.

We pick them up, and Dad drives since he's the only one who hasn't been drinking. It's a tight squeeze in his car, so I pull Veronica onto my lap. We're both a lot more comfortable since we ran inside to change out of our costumes.

We drop Noble and Jani off and a few minutes later, we're all seated around a table in the twenty-four-hour restaurant. At least it's not near three a.m. yet, when the drunks pour in from the local bars.

Everyone is pretty much sobering up, especially after we dig into the food. Bailey and Aiden giggle and draw on the kid's placemats with crayons in between bites of pancakes. Mom and Dad laugh and chat with Veronica, while she fills Dad in on their night's adventure. Maybe I'm getting old, but this is more my idea of fun.

Gathered together, enjoying each other. This is family, and that now includes Veronica and Aiden, whether we ever seal the deal with a marriage or not. By the time we're finished eating, Aiden is asleep with his head in Bailey's lap, and Bailey's eyes are drooping as well.

Veronica reaches to wake Aiden as we get ready to leave, but I stop her. "I've got him," I tell her, scooping him up and carrying him to the car. He doesn't stir as he's strapped into his booster seat.

That's one of those memories I love from being a kid. Being asleep in the back seat of the car and waking up in my bed. It was like teleporting. Aiden's warm weight in my arms as I carry him upstairs and tuck him into his bed reminds me of doing the same with Bailey. I always wanted a son as well, and now I have one.

One look at Veronica's face when she comes in from work, and I know she's had a bad day. The kids are playing in the backyard when I take a seat beside her on the couch.

"They're selling the hotel. And the next people plan to staff it with friends and family. I have a month to find a new job."

I wrap my arm around her. "I'm sorry. I know it wasn't your favorite place, but you've been with them for a long time."

"Yeah, I'm not pissed at the owners. They have every right to sell, and they're giving me three month's severance pay, but I hate to start over somewhere new."

Seizing my opportunity, I remind her. "You enjoyed filling in for Margo when she first went on maternity leave. She's decided to be a stay at home mom, and my temporary employee couldn't sell snow cones in hell. Come and work with me."

She scoffs, dropping a quick kiss on my jaw. "You mean come and work for you. I don't think that's a good idea."

"You promised to marry me after one year."

"I did." She grins up at me.

"So, then you'll just be working for our family business, not as your boyfriend's employee. If you need another incentive to be my wife." I run my palm down my bare chest. "I mean, you're already getting all this."

Her fingers pick at the seam of her jeans as she thinks about it. "Do you know why I wanted to wait a year?"

"In case I don't age well?"

She laughs and rubs a finger over the stubble on my cheek, where a bit of gray is starting to mix in. "I had a few accounts go to collection, medical bills from Aiden's birth and childhood that I was still paying on. They tanked my credit. After all you've done to get your finances straight, I wasn't going to let mine drag you down." She lays a finger over my lips when I start to argue. "But, with this severance, I'll have them covered."

"Does that mean..."

"If you still want to get the government involved, I'd love to be your wife."

From bad news to the best fucking news in the world.

I practically dive on top of her, pinning her under me on the couch, and kiss her giggling mouth. "It's about damn time. Are you going to work with me?"

"Anything but doing windows," she laughs.

The back door slams shut and Aiden's voice rings out. "Gross! They're kissing!"

Laughing, we sit up, and Veronica gives me a small nod. "That's what people do when they're going to get married," I tell him.

Bailey squeals and leaps onto the sofa next to Veronica. "Really?"

"If you'll be my maid of honor." Bailey hugs her with the biggest smile I've ever seen on her face.

Aiden hasn't said anything yet. He stands in front of us, looking uncertain.

"What do you think, A?" I ask.

He chews his lip and asks, "Do I have to wear a tie?"

All three of us laugh at his main concern. "No, buddy, we won't make you wear a tie."

"Will you be my dad, then?"

Silence reigns, and he fidgets as I soften my voice to ask, "Do you want me to be your dad?"

His little face is serious as he responds. "I think you already are my dad. Because Eddie says that dads teach you how to ride a bike, and help you with schoolwork, and keep your secrets. Like when I broke that glass, and you told Mom you did it. Or when I pooped the bed and you washed the sheet before anyone could see."

His eyes suddenly widen as he realizes he's just told on himself. Before he can regret any of it, I grab him in a bear hug.

This kid.

My kids.

My family.

They're fucking everything.

"You're right, buddy. I'm already your dad."

Epilogue

One year later

Neal

"Closing early today?" Harrison asks, nodding at the sign outside Jetsky's. He's brought in his weekly cars that he's just acquired as trade ins.

"Yeah, it can't be helped. Veronica and I have to be in court at three."

"Did you rob a bank, or have you been prostituting yourself again?" Harrison cracks up at his own joke.

"Don't hate me because I'm beautiful, old man." He chuckles as I go on to explain. "I filed to adopt Aiden, and Veronica did the same for Bailey. The adoptions are being finalized today. We'll both officially be the legal parents of both kids."

Harrison beams and shakes my hand. "Well, congratulations! You have a beautiful family."

"Thank you."

"And I have a beautiful new SUV crossover that I'm sure you'd all love." There it is. The sales pitch.

Laughing, I nod. "Actually, Harrison, I am looking for a new vehicle. Why don't I come in on Monday, and you can show me what you have?"

"That's what I like to hear! I knew I'd wear you down

eventually." He slaps me on the back.

"Just shy of ten years, man. Killer skills," I taunt.

Greg, the kid whose job is to drive the cars onto the track, jumps into his last one and pulls it around. "I'd better get moving. I'll see you Monday."

"No minivans," I caution him. "I still have a penis."

He throws back his head, and I can hear his laughter all the way across the lot as he makes his way inside.

Veronica walks up to me with a smile. "What did you tell him?"

"That we're shopping for a new car. Made his day."

"Clearly."

Two hearses pull in and stop next to the vacuums, and the look of dread on Greg's face as he approaches them makes me hide a smile. The funeral home is one of our newer accounts. After they deliver the coffin to the graveyard, they come to us to get the dead flowers vacuumed up, and the hearses washed and ready for the next procession.

The kids are endlessly amused by the creepy cars, but Greg doesn't see the humor. Aiden and Bailey show up just in time to see the hearses pull in.

"Aiden was eager to go," Bailey explains, as he rushes up to me. Bailey has been watching him at home all day and I'm sure she's been asked if it's time to go a million times.

"No problem, these are our last two." I motion for another employee to put up the cones to block the driveway entrance.

"Are there dead guys in there?" Aiden asks, excited, pressing his face against the tinted glass.

Greg gives us all a look as he quickly sweeps out the back, between the runners where the caskets are placed.

"Nope, no dead guy," I tell him.

Harrison is waving at me from the front corner of the building, so Veronica keeps an eye on things while I head to see what the issue is.

One of the cars he's brought in won't start, so I grab my battery jumper and have him on his way in a few minutes. The first hearse is pulled out by an employee, and the others jump to wipe it down, so I walk inside to see if the other one is about finished.

Now, usually, no one rides through with the car, unless there's some reason or the owner prefers it, so I'm a little surprised to see Greg sitting bolt upright in the driver's seat as the hearse is being pulled through the brushes and water. He looks like he'd rather be anywhere else in the world.

As I'm watching through the glass, and just as the hearse is reaching the end of the track where it'll be stopped by a rubber bumper, I see him freak the fuck out. I don't know what just happened, but the boy is seriously losing his shit, bouncing around the front seat until he finally jumps out and runs away like it's on fire.

My first thought was that a wasp or bee got in with him and he was getting stung. But when I rush into the garage to see what happened, two different creatures climb out of the back of the hearse, laughing so hard they can't speak.

"What the hell did you two do?" I ask Bailey and Aiden as Veronica approaches from behind me.

"A-Aiden slammed his hands onto the glass partition and smashed his face against it, growling like a z-zombie," she gasps, holding her stomach as her laughter intensifies.

Yeah, those would be my kids that climbed into the back of the hearse while Greg wasn't watching, waited until he was trapped by the brushes with no way to escape, then scared the living shit out of him.

Aiden runs over to Veronica, still giggling. "I scared him good, Mom, did you see?"

"He yelled help!" Bailey snorts. "Like, who was he yelling at?" She sits on the top of a plastic soap barrel, trying to catch her breath as laughter pours out of her.

When I look to Veronica for help, something occurs to me. "Why did he ride through with it in the first place?"

Aiden grins. "Mom told him the man wanted him to."

I should've known she was in on it. When I raise my eyebrows and meet her gaze, her laughter spills out, and she shrugs. "He sprayed us with the hose. Totally had it coming."

Greg approaches in time to hear her and raises his hands in front of him. "Truce! No more pranks!"

"What did you think was back there?" I ask, trying not to laugh.

"I didn't know and wasn't about to find out."

By the time we have the final hearse dried off and returned to the owner, it's time to head to court.

We've been told today is just a formality. All the papers have been signed. Both Aiden's biological father and Bailey's biological mother signed over their rights with no arguments, and neither showed up at the past court dates.

Still, it's a relief to hear the judge announce that we are now their legal parents. We don't hear those words alone, not by a long shot. My parents are there, and pretty much everyone from Violent Circle.

Violent Circle isn't such a bad place to live now. After the threats from the Housing Department and the scathing report by the local news, the new management quickly retracted its former regulations. The money paid by tenants to reclaim the toys and bikes stolen from them was returned, and the owners were put on probation by the Housing Department. The tenants all know how to contact them if management steps over that line.

I was so glad I could help make things better before we moved. We smile back at the crowd of neighbors, friends, and family, gathered at the back of the courtroom, all so happy for us and our kids.

"I can see you have a very large and loving support system," the judge says, after his pronouncement.

"Yes sir, one big family," Veronica replies.

Thanks for reading! If you'd like to check out more of my work, I have two books that are always free!

Everly, Book one of The Striking Back Series
And
Landon, Book one of The In Safe Hands Series:

Acknowledgements

This may be my favorite of the books I've written, mainly because I got to use so much of the stuff that came out of my son's mouth when he was Aiden's age. I'm sure any mother of boys can relate.

Of course, this book couldn't have happened without all the support I get from the book community and these awesome people. First, I'd like to thank my PA, Melissa Teo, who puts up with my weird, middle-of-the-night messages when I'm stuck, frustrated, or just need an opinion. She runs an amazing book group where I spend far too much time. So, if it's taking me too long to get a book out, it's her fault.

You can yell at her here, but be sure to stick around because it's an amazing group to belong to. B.A.N.G.

https://www.facebook.com/groups/BookSmackedBangers/

To my betas, who make sure my books aren't riddled with mistakes and typos, you guys make me look so much smarter than I am. Thanks so much, Veronica Ashley, Paige Sayer, Colette Trainor, Aimee Degagne, Amanda Munson, Theresa O'Reilly, and Bridget McEvoy.

The cover of Clean Start was created by Ally Hastings, of Starcrossed Covers. Thanks so much, Ally. Not every designer would take a request like putting a toilet brush on the cover and run with it.

https://www.facebook.com/groups/256219801390173

To my group, the Shady Ladies. You have no idea how much your encouragement and support push me to make my books the best they can be. Thanks for making the group such a fun, drama free place to hang out, for getting my sense of humor, and not thinking I'm crazy. Or at least keeping it to yourself if you do. http://www.facebook.com/groups/shadyladiesplace

Last, but certainly not least, thanks to all the book bloggers, page owners, and group owners who work tirelessly to help me and so many other authors get their stories out there. We couldn't do any of this without you.

Stalking Links

I love to connect with readers! Please stalk me at the following links:
Friend me at:
https://facebook.com/authorsmshade

Like my page:
https://facebook.com/smshadebooks

Follow on Twitter:
https://twitter.com/authorSMShade

Visit my blog:
http://www.smshade.blogspot.com

Sign up for my monthly newsletter:
http://bit.ly/1zNe5zu

Would you like to be a part of the S.M. Shade Book Club? As a member, you'll be entered in giveaways for gift cards, e-books, and Advanced Read Copies. Be a part of the private Facebook group and privy to excerpts and cover art of upcoming books before the public. You can request to join at: https://facebook.com/groups/694215440670693

More by S.M. Shade

The Striking Back Series

Book 1: Everly

The first time I met Mason Reed, we were standing naked in a bank, surrounded by guns.

That should have been a warning.

An MMA champion, trainer, and philanthropist, but not a man who gives up easily, Mason is trouble dipped in ink and covered in muscle.

Growing up in foster care, I'm well aware that relationships are temporary, and I do my best to avoid them. After a sheet clenching one night stand, I'm happy to move on, but Mason pursues me relentlessly. Sweet, caring, protective, and at times, a bossy control freak, this persistent man has climbed inside my heart, and I can't seem to shake him.

After saving me from a life threatening situation, he's also won something much harder to obtain. My trust. But does he deserve it? Is his true face the one he shows the world? Or is his charitable, loving manner only a thin veneer?

This book contains sexual situations and is intended for ages 18 and older.

Book 2: Mason

From the moment I saw her, I wanted her in my bed.

I should've stopped there.

Everly Hall burst into my complicated life and changed it forever. I'm a fighter, but I had no defense against this beautiful, stubborn woman.

Now, I stand to lose everything I have, everything I am. My secrets are dangerous, and put more lives at stake than my own. I intended to tell her in time, but my time is up.

Everything rests on Everly.

This is the conclusion of Mason and Everly's story.

Contains violence and sexual situations and is intended for adults 18 and older.

Book 3: Parker

Hit it and quit it.

One and done.

Hump and dump.

That has been my philosophy on relationships for the last seven years. Don't get me wrong, I'm not a bad guy. I'm always upfront and truthful with the women I date. I don't promise them anything but a good time.

I could've gone on happily sleeping my way through the major metropolitan area if it wasn't for her. The dark haired beauty who haunts my days and keeps me awake at night. Strong and sweet, she makes me reconsider everything I believe about love.

Too bad she's completely off limits.

I've never been good at following the rules.

Book 4: Alex – An M/M Romance

Ninety- two days. Thirteen weeks. That's how long it's been since I lost my love, my best friend. It's been everything I can do to drag myself out of bed and get back to work, but I know Cooper would want me to move on. I think he'd even be happy if he knew who I want to move on with. The target of my affection, though, may not be so thrilled about my choice.

He's straight. Or he thinks he is.

A womanizer of the worst kind with a face and body that keeps a steady stream of willing women at his door, he seems happy to work his way through the entire female population. But there's no mistaking the way he looks at me when he thinks I'm not paying attention.

One way or another, I'll show him what he really wants.

This is book four of The Striking Back Series, but can also be read as a standalone novel.

Intended for 18 years and older. Contains sexual content, including sex between two men.

The In Safe Hands Series

Landon, Book One

Zoe

I'm not interested. I'm not interested in his blue-green ocean colored eyes, his lean muscular body, or that crooked smile that can be so infuriating. I have more important things to worry about, like how to keep myself in college and my sixteen year old brother fed and sheltered. We all know life is hard, some of us just learn that lesson younger than others, but that doesn't mean I'll give up. I intend to succeed and make sure my brother has the opportunities he deserves, and no privileged jerk is going to distract me.

Landon

I don't date. Don't get me wrong, I'm far from celibate, but my condition makes carrying on any kind of normal relationship impossible. My life revolves around In Safe Hands or ISH, the underground hacker group I work with to track down and take care of predators and sex offenders who beat the system. I'm satisfied with my life until the day I meet the smart mouthed, compassionate, determined woman who opens my eyes to possibilities I never thought existed.

Dare, Book Two

Ayda

I hear him.

His deep voice and rumbling laugh. The bang of the headboard slamming the wall and fake screams from yet another woman. Derek is a pile of muscle and ink, a bad boy fantasy only a few layers of wood and plaster away. It's all I expect or want him to be.

Until that irresistible voice begins talking to me.

Dare

I hear her.

The clicking of her fingers on a keyboard, her music or TV playing in the background. Her musical laugh and soft cries of pleasure, accompanied by a low, steady buzz. Ayda is a good girl who keeps to herself, and I have no business pursuing her, but I'm not a man known for doing the right thing.

I'm an ex-con. I'm a criminal.

And I want her.

Justus, Book Three

Justus

I'm not conceited.

Really, I'm not. It just so happens I have a body a Greek God would be jealous of, and a face that could make an angel weep. Other than that, I'm just your everyday normal guy who happens to take his clothes off for money. Sure, I've had to dispose of a few guys for In Safe Hands, the organization I work for that helps track predators and child molesters, but other than that, completely normal.

Women flock to me, screaming and paying for the right to touch me, so why is this woman so stubborn? Sadie Belmont's curvy body and sharp tongue have haunted me since I met her a year ago. There's something about her that gets stuck in my head like a bad song, and I'm determined to find out why I want her so badly, and why she can't stomach the thought.

Sadie

I can't believe I'm doing this. Of all the men in the world, I'm taking Justus Alexander to my childhood home in Oklahoma to meet my mother. A stripper who has a revolving door of women jumping in and out of his bed. Nine months ago when I lied to my mother and told her I had a steady boyfriend, I didn't expect it to come to this. She doesn't have long to live, and her only wish is to know I have a husband before she goes.

I can't disappoint her, and male escorts cost way more than I can afford, so when Justus volunteered, I took him up on his offer. I know what he wants. After annoying me with constant pick up lines for a year, he sees an opportunity to get me in bed. It's not going to happen. I just need to get through this week with my sanity intact.

Tucker, Book Four

Tucker

She's beautiful.

She's young.

She's driving me out of my mind.

I've always done my best to avoid Leah Bolt. I have enough problems without having to deal with a young woman with a crush. My life has been a disaster since I was court-martialed and dishonorably discharged from the military. After spending a year living on the streets, I'm finally starting to pull things together.

Now, I'm stuck with her, living side by side in my house with my complete opposite. If spending every day with this peppy, optimistic, energetic woman doesn't kill me, her brother will. Dare is a friend and a member of In Safe Hands, a group that tracks down sexual predators and brings them to justice. He has also done time and is the size of a mountain.

I've survived combat, but I may be taken down by a perky blond.

Leah

He's gorgeous.

He's older.

He's a stubborn, broody jerk.

Tucker Long is every woman's dream...until you talk to him. He may be sexy when he's out sweating in the sun with sawdust clinging to him as he hammers and saws, but try to hold a conversation and all you get are grunts and nods.

He was the one who wanted a house sitter and just because his plans fell through doesn't mean I'm changing mine. My future is up in the air while I try to decide who I want to be, and Tucker's farm is the perfect place for me to do it. He calls me kid, but the way he looks at me doesn't lie.

I may be ten years younger, but I can still handle him.

All that Remains – An MMF Menage Trilogy

The Last Woman, All That Remains: Book One

When Abby Bailey meets former model and actor, Airen Holder, in a darkened department store, romance is the last thing on her mind. A plague has decimated the population, leaving Abby to raise her son alone in a world without electricity, clean water, or medical care. Her only priority is survival.

Traumatized by the horror of the past months, Abby and Airen become a source of comfort for one another. Damaged by her past and convinced Airen is out of her league, Abby is determined to keep their relationship platonic. However, Airen is a hard man to resist, especially after he risks his life to save hers.

When a man named Joseph falls unconscious in their yard, and Abby nurses him back to health, everything changes. How does love differ in this new post-apocalyptic world? Can three unlikely survivors live long enough to find their place in it?

This is the first of the All that Remains series and can also be read as a stand alone novel. It contains violence and sexual situations and is recommended for ages 18 and older.

Falling Together, All That Remains: Book Two

In the aftermath of a global nightmare, Abby Holder is living her dream. Married to the love of her life, Airen, and surrounded by friends and family, it seems she's found her happily ever after.

But the struggle of living in a post-plague world is never ending. When circumstances take Airen far away, she's faced with the devastating realization he may be lost to her forever. Broken-hearted, she turns to Joseph, her best friend and the only one who understands her pain. After all, he loves Airen too.

The sound of a car horn in the middle of the night changes everything, leaving Abby caught between the two most important men in her life. After surviving the worst the world could throw at them, Airen, Abby, and Joseph must face the most brutal human experience...true love. Can they overcome the betrayal, the hurt feelings, and jealousy to do what's right for the ones they love?

Their circumstances are far from ordinary. Perhaps the answer is extraordinary as well.

This book includes sexual scenes between two men and is intended for ages 18 and older

Infinite Ties, All That Remains: Book Three

The more you look to the future, the more the past pursues you.

Abby, Airen, and Joseph have fought and suffered to come together. All they want is to move forward and raise their family with the love they never had.

Unfortunately, the re-appearance of former friends and enemies complicates their lives, threatening to expose closely guarded secrets. With a vital rescue looming, their relationship isn't the only thing at risk. Can they let go of the past in order to hang on to a future with each other?